Murder

on the

Moors

Book 4

A Dodo Dorchester Mystery
by

Ann Sutton

Published by

Wild Poppy Publishing LLC
Highland, UT 84003

Distributed by Wild Poppy Publishing

Cover design by Julie Matern
Cover Design ©2021 Wild Poppy Publishing LLC

Edited by Jolene Perry

In Memory of Matthew Matern

Table of Contents

The black and white image flickered in the dark, smoky cinema as the elderly pianist dramatically crashed the keys of the old piano.

Dodo sneezed as the beautiful heroine finally kissed her long-lost love. Her eyes brimmed over with tears that had little to do with the action on the screen. Beside her, Lizzie was sniffing into a sizable handkerchief. The pianist's melodious music descended into a light, haunting melody that charged the picture house with the perfect ambience for the passionate, on-screen kiss.

The warm room plunged into further darkness as the image faded to a small white dot, and 'The End' was displayed.

Dodo sighed, her heart twisting in her chest, and dabbed her eyes as the house lights went up. Looking around, she saw that every woman in the room was overcome by the story they had just seen. This had been the perfect way to wallow in her own private misery.

"Ooh, that was lovely," sighed Lizzie, making no attempt to move from her seat. "That Monte Blue is so handsome. Don't you agree m'lady?"

Dodo was folding her damp, lacy handkerchief and placing it in her soft, leather handbag. "Dreamy," she agreed.

Ever since breaking things off with the oh-so-suitable Charlie Chadwick, Dodo had felt off-kilter. But the split had been the right thing to do. He deserved someone more devoted. Someone whose heart was more faithful. And to make things more complicated, the person who *had* stolen her heart was decidedly off limits.

Feeling the need to bask in her dark mood, she had chosen the romantic drama film as the perfect indulgence. And since her sister, Didi, was out of town, she had convinced Lizzie, her lady's maid, to accompany her. She had not taken much persuading.

The film had been just the right mix of melodrama and love-story, both lifting her aching soul to soaring heights and sending it crashing to bottomless depths of despondency. In fact, it mirrored her own recent life experience quite perfectly.

Except for the happy ending.

"I could sit here all day savoring these happy feelings," said Lizzie, her moist eyes wistful.

"Me too. Hollywood has excelled at exploiting the tender hearts of women so that we hand over our money again and again. It is quite brilliant."

The usherettes appeared without their confectionary goodies.

"But I think we are being encouraged to leave." Dodo tipped her head to indicate the girls in the black and white uniforms. Lizzie gathered up her capacious handbag, stuffed her handkerchief in it, and enjoyed one last sniff.

When they reached the top of the stairs, the black, baize doors opened, and Dodo squinted in the harsh sunlight. She pulled down the front of her maroon hat to shield her eyes from the glare.

"Let's go to Claridge's for a cream tea! It is the perfect ending to this day of tribute to unattainable hedonism," she declared.

Lizzie looked askance. "I wouldn't feel comfortable there m'lady."

"Nonsense!" cried Dodo, throwing a pearl white, cashmere scarf around her long neck.

"It might be nonsense to you but there would be a lot of raised eyebrows—it would put me off my scones." Lizzie's brows were pinched into a deep 'v'.

Dodo dragged down her bottom lip. "Oh, well if you put it like that." They walked out into the chill of late autumn and she raised her hand to hail a taxi. "How about a Lyon's tea house then?"

"Oh yes!" cried Lizzie who was partial to teashops. "Much more suitable for me, but a bit of a come-down for you, m'lady." The maid's eyes were twinkling with mischief.

Dodo stopped watching traffic and stared at her maid. "Am I that much of a snob, Lizzie?"

"I refuse to answer that question on the grounds that it may incriminate me," Lizzie replied with a grin.

A taxi pulled up to the curb and they both jumped in.

"Lyon's tea house, Piccadilly," Dodo told the cabbie.

"Right you are, miss."

As the cab lurched away, Dodo crossed her hands over her lap.

"It *was* a splendid film, wasn't it? My heart is still tingling."

"So romantic!" agreed Lizzie. "And the actors were all terribly glamorous. I could watch it every day for a week," she confessed. She looked sidelong at her mistress. "Did it make you feel any better, m'lady?"

Dodo considered the question, gripping her chin. "Honestly? For about five minutes but as soon as it was over the wretchedness returned."

"Perhaps you will change your mind about Mr. Charlie after a while," said Lizzie. "He is such a lovely man. Take some time apart. They say absence makes the heart grow fonder."

Dodo had been unable to admit to Lizzie all the reasons she had broken things off with Charlie Chadwick. She had not even told her sister. The real truth was that a certain Scotland Yard detective had captured her heart in a way she could not ignore, but a romance with him was out of the question. Earl's daughters did not engage in relationships with policemen. However, her undeniable attraction to Chief Inspector Blood had highlighted the fact that she did not feel the same way about Charlie. She had split up with him because it was unfair not to.

Taking a breath deep enough to swim clear across a pool, she merely said, "Not in this case."

"Well then. If that's how you feel, I won't say another word about it. None of my business anyway."

The manner in which Lizzie was gripping the handles of her handbag told another story. Dodo was certain that Lizzie was positively drunk with curiosity about the whole matter, but as close as they were, she could not bring herself to admit the embarrassing truth. Not yet anyway.

"As much as I like Mr. Charlie, there are plenty of other fish in the sea," continued Lizzie. "And just look at you! Men fall all over themselves to get your attention."

Dodo pulled out her compact mirror and checked her lipstick.

Parting company with Charlie had been right but disappointing the thoroughly charming man had almost broken her, and she had settled into this well-deserved depression. And of course, there was the unspoken fact that she had been forced to walk away from a man she was falling in love with.

Life could be very complicated.

Staring out the window of the taxi, lost in her own thoughts, Dodo was surprised when the driver declared, "Lyon's!" and pulled to the curb.

Dodo threw him some money and they stepped out. The light was fast fading and the Lyon's corner store, with its patented white and gold sign, beckoned to them. Perhaps she could further drown her sorrows in clotted cream and strawberry jam.

A 'nippy' welcomed them at the door in her starched cap, black dress, and white apron, chattering pleasantries as they followed her to an empty place in the crowded restaurant. The waitresses were nicknamed 'nippies' because they darted quickly from table to table.

The pleasant scent of baking scones filled the air.

"Two cream teas, please," said Dodo as they settled themselves at a shiny, gold trimmed table.

"Perhaps you could get a job here," said Lizzie, laughing as the pretty girl left. "I hear eight hundred nippies got married last year."

Dodo rolled her eyes.

It was well known that only beautiful girls were hired for the job because this attracted single men to visit the establishments in droves. It was hardly surprising that marriages were the result.

"What time is the train to Devon tomorrow?" asked Lizzie, taking off her gloves and slipping them into her bag. Dodo was sure every gadget known to man was contained in it.

"Eleven-thirty with a connection at Paddington."

"A change of scenery is just what you need," Lizzie remarked. "It's always good to get away after disappointed love."

Dodo frowned. "And how many times have you had your heart broken?"

4

Lizzie wrinkled her nose. "Does Collin Bradshaw in primary school count?"

Crossing her arms, Dodo dipped her chin. "No."

"Then none. But that's what my sisters say."

Dodo looked around the busy restaurant. Nippies hurried, while balancing tea trays and notebooks. Each wall of the corner structure was made up of large windows that looked out onto the crowded, wet street.

"You'll enjoy some time with your cousins," added Lizzie.

Dodo's cousins were fraternal twins who were always getting into trouble when they were children. Esmerelda and Bartholomew Gillingsworth. They were so awful in their youth that they had scared their poor mother into refusing to bear any more offspring. Every visit to Dartmoor as children had been an adventure for Dodo and her sister.

The twins had mellowed with age but by the time their mother had decided that they were quite pleasant company, and that one or two more might be tolerable, her husband had died. Now, Bartie was Lord Gillingsworth.

Their rambling, gothic-styled estate perched on the edge of Dartmoor, offered unobstructed views of the wild landscape—when it was not shrouded in the infamous moor fog. It had both thrilled and terrified Dodo as a child.

"Yes," she agreed. "They will be the perfect antidote to my current malaise." She rested her chin in her hand and pouted, remembering her beloved cousins.

"Do you know any of the other people who will be going?" asked Lizzie, fluffing her damp hair.

"Bunty was a bit vague on that matter," Dodo admitted. "I'd rather no one else was going at all but it can't be helped. I just needed to get away. When she told me there were some others invited, I wasn't too bothered. She won't care if I'm not very sociable. I am definitely not in the market for a man at this point."

"Uh huh," said Lizzie, eyes crinkling.

"I'm not!" cried Dodo. "I'm emotionally exhausted and I just need a break."

"Flies to honey it is with you, m'lady. Flies to honey."

5

"It is very nice of you to say that dear, but I insist that I have no interest in romance. I'm looking forward to healthy walks on the moors, burying my nose in books and fashion magazines, and eating myself silly." The Gillingsworths had an excellent cook who was a favorite of Dodo's.

"Bunty," Lizzie said as she drummed her fingers on the table, waiting for the nippy's return. "It sounds nothing like Esmerelda. How did she get the nickname?"

"She hated the name Esmerelda with a passion and quite honestly, it doesn't suit her at all," began Dodo. "She read the name 'Bunty' in a book when she was five and announced at tea that she would no longer answer to the name she was given at birth, instead commanding everyone to call her 'Bunty' from that day forth."

The nippy returned with their tea and a plate overflowing with scones. Dodo realized she was starving. Grabbing a spoon, she dug into the bowl of strawberry jam, spreading it on the scone and then took a generous portion of the stiff, clotted cream and slathered it over the top.

Sinking her teeth into the delicious concoction, she groaned with pleasure.

"This might be my favorite food," she declared.

"What about French croissants dipped in hot chocolate?" asked Lizzie, helping herself to a healthy amount of the pale, thick cream.

Dodo bit her scarlet lip. "Oof. I think this wins by a whisker."

Chapter 2

Blackwood Manor rose up in the foggy dark like the shadow of a vampire bat in a cave. Tonight, the sprawling eighteenth-century structure came complete with menacing, swirling mists around its sharp turrets, and the hoot of owls. All that was missing was a witch on a broomstick.

Dodo felt a familiar thrill as the car crunched onto the gravel driveway.

The ramshackle house had the interesting capacity to appear charming and quintessentially English in the daytime, and terrifyingly spooky at night.

"Ooooh! I forget how scary this place is," groaned a wide-eyed Lizzie as they exited the taxi. "It's like the backdrop for a thriller at the theater."

"An apt description, my dear," said Dodo with a grin. "Just remember how welcoming it looks in the daylight. And think of the inhabitants. You couldn't ask for friendlier hosts."

Before she finished speaking, the heavy, oak front door creaked open and comforting, warm light spilled onto the cracked stone steps as one tall and one short shadow filled the space.

"Dodo!" Bunty lumbered down the stairs, her long limbs slowing her down as her lithe brother sprang down the steps like a hunting dog. Bartholomew Gillingsworth III wrapped Dodo's delicate hand in his, and pulled her in for a chaste kiss on the cheek.

"You smell delicious, Dodo!" he declared. "And who is this vision of loveliness?"

Dodo tried to hide a smile as Lizzie flushed to her blonde roots. Bartie always was prone to theatrics.

"Mr. Bartholomew," Lizzie gushed, "you are an incorrigible flatterer."

Bunty wrapped her long arms around Dodo and lifted her from the ground, her frizzy hair tickling Dodo's cheek.

"Bunty!" Dodo cried, "I am not a five-year-old!"

"I know but it is so fun to act like one! Don't you agree?"
She set Dodo back onto the gravel driveway as Dodo righted her
hat and pulled down her fine, wool skirt.

"Come on in," said Bartie, grabbing Dodo by the hand and
dragging her up the mossy steps. "It's far too cold out here."

Dodo's heels were not suitable for the precipitous flight,
and she almost twisted her ankle. "Slow down, Bartie! I don't want
to be laid up with a sprain all week."

He puckered his lips and released her hands. "Sorry, old
thing. It is just too marvelous to see you. Too bad Didi couldn't
come." He ascended the steps backwards. "What is it? About two
years since you've been down?"

Lizzie pushed into the hall followed by Bunty bringing up
the rear, who kicked the door closed with one enormous shoe while
pushing her hands through the straggly, brown curls.

One of the twins' many idiosyncrasies was that though they
were rich enough, they chose to live life simply. They could easily
afford a whole brigade of servants but preferred not. Hence, there
were no under footmen, no butler, no flotilla of housemaids.
Instead, they ran their ship on a skeleton staff—people they knew
and trusted.

Dodo looked around the familiar, dirty vestibule. Another
consequence of this relaxed attitude to life was that Blackwood
Manor was a little bit frayed around the edges and not usually
spotlessly clean. In fact, it was the opposite. These things just
didn't matter to the Gillingsworths. They did not stand on
ceremony and didn't expect their guests to either. Bartie's
philosophy was that a man should feel at ease in his own home.

"This way!" Bunty commanded, leading the way through
the cavernous hall to a battered door.

Lizzie hesitated.

"Goodness girl! Come on in!" barked Bartie. "There will be
plenty of time to get settled
in downstairs later. You must both be starving. We're having
toasted crumpets by the fire."

Dodo laughed and nudged Lizzie's elbow to follow Bartie.
Lord Gillingsworth treated

everyone the same. It was one of the many things she loved about him. Lowly housemaid or Queen of England—it didn't matter. It went against the societal grain, but it was so refreshing.

"If you're sure," said Lizzie haltingly.

Bartie lifted a short finger and pointed it at the ceiling. "I am the Lord of this manor and it's an order!"

"Oh, alright then," said Lizzie, her pink cheeks betraying that she was delighted to be included.

A roaring fire was in the enormous fireplace and Dodo was transported back to tea in this very room after days spent fishing on the pond, and roaming the moors with the dogs, hunting for the wild Dartmoor ponies that had lived in the area for thousands of years. The vast room, with its oak rafters and deer's head trophies was as familiar and comforting as a childhood blanket.

And as hot as a furnace.

Dodo pulled off the fine wool scarf from around her neck and slipped out of her coat.

An ancient, tapestry sofa was pulled close to the flames, along with two threadbare armchairs. At the present, one of the chairs was occupied by an aging basset hound.

"Herbert!" yelled Bartie. "Off the furniture!" The lazy dog opened one sorry eye, looked around and then snapped it shut. Bartie offered them a squashed smile that almost reached his ears then pushed the offending animal slowly off the chair, brushing the hairy fabric with his hand. The dog slunk behind the couch and curled up with a graying golden retriever.

"Miss Lizzie. Please, sit here. Excuse the dog hair." He patted the seat and a cloud of dust puffed into the air. Lizzie wrinkled her nose.

Bunty sat as close to the fire as possible without catching alight and put her hand on the seat beside her. "Dodo, come and sit by me on the sofa."

Dodo sat down and was immediately engulfed in a kiln quality heat. She shed her jacket and cardigan. Amazingly, Bunty was still wrapped in a moth-eaten jumper whose sleeves did not quite reach her wrists. Everything about Blackwood was in a state of delightful decay—including its owners.

"Here!" she said, handing Dodo a blackened poker with one hand and a crumpet with the other. "Stick this on the end and hold it to the fire. Careful though, cooks pretty dashed quickly."

I can't imagine why?

Dodo happily did as she was told and felt a wave of heat fan her face. She wiped a wrist across her forehead.

Bartie was handing Lizzie a crumpet and poker. She glanced at Dodo, excitement flashing in her eyes.

"How was the train?" asked Bunty, lavishing butter on a toasted crumpet. Dodo watched as it melted onto her cousin's raggedy tartan skirt. Bunty dragged a long finger through it and stuck it in her mouth, closing her eyes in apparent ecstasy. She had a knack for finding joy in the simple things of life.

"Not too bad," said Dodo, rescuing her own smoking crumpet a fraction too late. "Though there was a funny old biddy in the restaurant car who talked non-stop while she was knitting. All I really wanted to do was keep my own company, but she would not take a hint." Bunty offered her the butter dish and Dodo took a liberal amount. "Said she knew you, I think. Jane someone or other. Has a nephew in the area."

Bartie winked at his twin sister. "That would be Chester's aunt. She comes down every couple of years or so. Dear old soul."

"Oh, I didn't mean she was ghastly," Dodo corrected herself. "I was just so awfully tired."

"Well, you can have a lovely rest here for a whole week," said Bunty, blinking like the owls Dodo could hear outside. "What's made you so tired anyway? You just mentioned troubles of the heart on the phone."

Lizzie's eyes widened. Dodo had been purposely circumspect with her cousins about the reason for her sudden visit.

"I was stepping out with a man who was falling in love with me, and I didn't reciprocate his feelings," explained Dodo.

"Oh, do elaborate," said Bunty. "I love to live vicariously when it comes to affairs of a romantic nature."

"Rubbish!" retorted Bartie with a chortle. "Don't believe a word of it, Dodo. One of the guests this weekend is her new beau."

"You have a beau?" This was a revelation as Bunty had never been comfortable around men she found attractive.

"Yes! Can you believe it! Me! You'll meet him tomorrow. I do hope you'll like him, Dodo. He's at least three inches taller than me," she gushed, "which is a miracle." Bunty topped the measuring tape at six feet.

Bunty rubbed her nose with the back of her hand. "But poor you. Tell me everything."

Dodo licked the remnants of butter from her fingers before beginning. "There's not much to tell," she lied, not wanting to rehash the whole sorry story. "I had the perfect man who was absolutely crazy about me, but I just didn't feel quite the same about him. He deserved better, so I broke it off. It was actually bally awful!"

"You must have liked him a bit or you wouldn't feel the need to slink away to the depths of Dartmoor," pointed out Bunty.

"Perceptive as always, Bunty," said Dodo, wiping some stray butter from her chin. "He was a friend first, and I feel just terrible about it all."

Bartie poked a finger through a hole in his sleeve. "Perhaps one of our guests will be able to help you forget him." An angelic grin lit up his boyish face. At twenty-five he could still easily have got into the county fair at half-price.

Dodo flung up her hands. "No! It's been quite a year for heartbreak. I'm not looking for any more romances."

The twins shared a glance and Dodo pretended she hadn't noticed.

"If you say so," said Bunty, narrowing her green eyes. "Now, who's for a tipple?"

Bartie went over to the drinks cabinet and poured them some cocktails while Lizzie excused herself to unpack for Dodo.

"She's a corker!" exclaimed Bartie as the door closed behind Lizzie.

"A national treasure," agreed Dodo. "And so much more than a maid."

"My maid just turned eighty-two," said Bunty sipping her drink. "She was mother's maid and she can't see very well anymore, or move fast for that matter, but I just don't have the heart to tell her it's time to retire. She never married and has no family left. We're all she has. I really don't need a maid at all, and thankfully, I never was very fussy about standards."

"No!" agreed Dodo.

She remembered once, when Bunty was twelve, she had come down to dinner with a duchess in her threadbare nightdress. Her mother had almost died with shame on the spot. The thought gave Dodo a stab of nostalgia for Aunt Winifred.

"So, who else is coming? You won't mind if I keep to myself, will you?"

"Of course not! Let's see," said Bunty putting one long finger to her chin. "Walter Montague. He's a chap we just met recently."

"He's a bit of an odd duck," said Bartie, "but good for a game of cards." He rubbed his nose with the back of his hand just like his sister. "Then there's Bunty's beau, Granville Post. He's a cricket player and a frightfully interesting chap."

Bunty's crooked smile divulged her enthusiasm for him. Dodo was more than intrigued.

"Isabella Dominguez," continued Bartie. "She's a Spanish opera singer. She's not terribly well known yet but I am sure she will be soon." A smile played on his lips.

"Granville asked me to invite her," explained Bunty. "He thinks her voice is exceptional and wants to be her patron." She was playing with a loose thread that was hanging from her skirt. "Who are we missing, Bartie?"

"Veronica Shufflebottom—"

"Oh no!" cried Dodo, gripping the arm of the sofa. "You can't be serious! I can't stand that woman! We have…a history."

Bartie leaned forward, fingers steepled, dark eyes shining with expectation behind the round lenses of his glasses. "Do tell."

Dodo's mouth twisted. "She's just the worst. An impossible human being. Catty, manipulative, a snitch. She made my life miserable at school. I hoped never to set eyes on her again."

"The cat! I had no idea," declared Bunty. "She never said she knew you. Well, it's too late to do anything about it now. How annoying."

Bunty pulled down the ratty jumper, her eyes full of compassion. "She's bringing someone. Don't remember his name. He plays polo. He should keep her out of your way."

"Let's hope so!"

Chapter 3

Dodo stood, arms out, eyes closed, drinking in the clean, fresh air as the raging wind tried to tear her hat from her bobbed hair.

Lizzie was still scrambling up the hill behind her, one hand clamped on the top of her hat, the other holding up her skirt as she maneuvered the uneven landscape.

"Good girl! Press on!" Dodo shouted, encouragingly.

Panting, Lizzie turned a grim glare on her mistress.

Dodo pulled down her lower lip.

As Lizzie climbed the last leg, huffing and puffing she pulled her coat collar away from her neck. "That is a lot steeper than it looks, m'lady."

Bunty had gone into town for supplies and Bartie had never been fond of rambling on the moors unless it was absolutely necessary. Hence, Lizzie had been commandeered into accompanying Dodo.

They both looked out across the harsh moors and memories of childhood adventures tumbled across Dodo's mind. The bracing breeze, filled with the scent of bogs, was knocking her head around like a prize boxer but it was also beginning to blow away the vestiges of guilt and sadness she had brought with her to Devon.

Gripped by a sudden need to yell, Dodo let out a primal howl that was grabbed by the boisterous wind and flung into the air.

"Ahhh!" screamed Lizzie, hand to her chest. "Could you warn me before calling on the hounds of hell?"

Dodo grinned. Lizzie's manners always slipped when she was surprised or frightened.

"I'm so sorry," she said. "I didn't know it was coming myself. It just felt so good to throw all that mess out of my head."

Lizzie pursed her lips. "If you don't mind me stating an opinion—"

"Not at all," Dodo assured her. "Unburden yourself."

"If you are this sad about breaking things off with Mr. Charlie, doesn't it mean you really liked him?"

Dodo scrunched up her nose. Perhaps it was time to tell Lizzie the whole story. She knew she could trust Lizzie to keep her secret.

Dodo faced into the view and the wind to avoid her maid's eye.

"It's not just Charlie."

Lizzie's head snapped round but Dodo kept her gaze straight ahead.

"Do you remember Chief Inspector Blood?" Her heart hiccupped as she said his name.

"The obnoxious one we met at Farrington Hall when the maid was murdered? The man who was so rude to you?"

Lizzie was not wrong in her description. The man had the social manners of a bull. But he also had an effect on Dodo that was unmatched.

"Yes. He worked the case at Ascot when Lord Barchester was murdered."

From the corner of her eye, she could see Lizzie frown.

"Ahh."

Dodo gathered up her courage and ploughed on. "We had a moment. A couple actually. Completely impossible, of course."

Lizzie remained uncharacteristically quiet as the wind continued to pummel them both.

Dodo let her eyes drift as far into the distance as possible. The long moor grass swayed in the wind like waves on the ocean.

After several minutes of avoidance, Dodo could stand it no longer.

"Say something, Lizzie," she cried over the punishing gale.

"What is there to say, m'lady? It is not possible for you to engage in a relationship with someone so far below you in station. End of story."

"But you must have opinions, surely?"

"I have plenty but I'm not sure it would be appropriate to share them." Her whole face puckered.

"In my defense, he improved on acquaintance," said Dodo. "He could actually be quite sweet. But you are quite right, such a relationship would be doomed. I was playing with fire, thinking I wouldn't get burned...but I did."

"What *were* you thinking?" asked Lizzie, her voice filled with incredulity. "What would your parents have said?"

"I wasn't thinking," Dodo confessed. "He made me feel all sorts of things I haven't ever felt. Exciting things. Things Charlie did not inspire in me. The contrast could not be ignored."

"Did he…" Lizzie hesitated, and Dodo could sense what was coming. "Did he kiss you?"

"No!" But she wished he had. "No, he inspired all those feelings without so much as a peck on the cheek. So, you see, I had to let Charlie go."

Lizzie nodded slowly, comprehension dawning. "And you have run away from the chief inspector too."

Lizzie turned her back to the view and the wind, securing her hat to prevent it being plucked from her head.

"Although I don't approve, I'm glad you told me," she said. "It all makes much more sense now."

"Don't approve?" asked Dodo, turning her back to the wind too.

"The classes shouldn't mix like that, m'lady. Never works."

§

The confession had drained Dodo emotionally and the hike had drained her physically—though both were therapeutic. Upon their return to the house, she had taken a short nap and awoken feeling lighter but chilly. Built in the early 1700's the house had seen few renovations and even fewer that involved modernization. She shivered. The big house was always drafty.

Making her way down to the drawing room, she hoped that the enormous fire had been stoked.

She flung open the door, expecting the room to be empty, and instead came face to face with a complete stranger. A man. A tall man with very large, discolored teeth and a thin beard.

"Oh, I'm terribly sorry!" she cried, stepping back, hands up as if in surrender.

"Think nothing of it." His voice was ridiculously plummy, almost exaggerated. "Walter Montague."

16

Dodo shrunk farther back from the ugly man, her hand firmly at her side. "Dodo Dorchester. Bunty's cousin."

Walter extended a wiry arm and clasped her unwilling hand in a firm shake. "Ah, I've heard a lot about you." He ran his muddy brown eyes over her as though she were a prize pig.

Dodo shuddered.

"In the society pages," he explained, placing his hands on his round middle. "I didn't hear Bunty say you were coming."

"That's because it is all rather last minute. I'm crashing the party, so to speak." She tried to step past him to the warmth of the fire but he was like a prison wall.

"Well, it is a welcome surprise." He brushed a lock of stringy, red hair out of his eyes.

"Thank you," she responded without really meaning it.

He finally moved aside, and she walked over to the fire, hands outstretched.

Walter followed her. "I just got here," he continued, settling his tall frame onto the battered couch. His long limbs were lanky in contrast to his thick mid-section. "Came by the ten o' clock train from Paddington and Bartie sent a car."

"I just got back from a walk on the moors. I'm freezing." She rubbed her hands together to emphasize her words.

"It *is* a rather blustery day." He reached an arm along the back of the sofa revealing a frayed cuff. Dodo stayed by the fire, turning her back to him.

"I know the twins from a card game I played a few weeks ago in Cornwall," he continued in his honking voice. "Bartie won a lot of money from me at cards. He was a good sport about it, though. I won it back from him the next day…still think he let me win. Jolly nice of him." His mobile, crowded mouth moved up, forcing his scraggly mustache to kiss his nose. Dodo scratched her own.

Finally warm, she sat in one of the decrepit armchairs. Herbert the dog occupied the other one.

She had chosen to wear wool trousers and an argyle sweater hoping to stave off the chill and they were absorbing the heat from the flames nicely.

17

Walter kicked out his large feet, crossing his legs at the ankles and making himself thoroughly at home. For reasons she could not put her finger on, his casualness did not sit well with her.

"What's the food like here?" he asked, running a finger around the inside of his ear.

Manners!

Since he had rubbed her the wrong way, she did not see any harm in teasing him.

"Awful! The cook is ninety-four and half blind. Be very careful of the fish—always finding bones in it. And she's rather heavy handed with the salt." This could not be further from the truth.

Walter's eyes bulged and his chin quivered sending ripples through the straggly red beard. "Thanks for the tip."

The elderly retriever struggled to its feet, tottered over to the fireplace, and sank down in front of the flames. Dodo leaned over and tickled him behind the ears. He grunted with pleasure.

Walter shifted along the sofa away from the animal. "Not fond of dogs," he explained.

A whoosh of air heralded the arrival of Bunty and Bartie and the awkward mood lightened.

"Ahh, you've met Walter," said Bunty, quirking an eyebrow at Dodo with a smirk that was hidden from Walter's line of sight.

"Yes!" he cried, in his annoying voice. "You didn't tell me there would be a celebrity among us."

Dodo clenched her jaw and tried to hitch a half-hearted smile but failed.

Bartie sat on the couch next to Walter and Bunty pushed the dog off the chair.

"How was the walk?" Bartie asked Dodo.

"Bracing. Blew all the cobwebs away." She tucked her hair behind her ear. "Well, almost all."

"Splendid. Glad you made it back before dark. It can be so dangerous out there when the light goes." Bartie's expression was curiously serious.

"I know!" Dodo exclaimed. "Do you remember that summer we stayed out too late and Bunty fell in a bog?" said Dodo.

"I will never forget it!" declared Bunty, her round, plain face charged with fear. "It was such a shock and so horribly cold."

"We almost fell in trying to get you out!" said Bartie, his young-looking features rigid at the memory. "And then we kept getting lost trying to find our way home."

"That was the last time we stayed out after sunset." Bunty rested her elbow on the side of the chair and leaned her chin on her fist, eyes somber.

The basset hound broke the mournful mood by barking sharply.

"Shush, Herbert!" commanded Bartie, but the dog just ignored him.

Shortly, a hubbub could be heard in the entry and two people entered the room. One was a tiny, doll-like girl with scarlet lips that matched her red dress, and raven hair, and the other was a youngish man who was so tall he looked like he had been carved out of a beech tree. His untidy face reminded Dodo of a lawn that needed a good mow—all bushy eyebrows and shaggy, pale hair.

Bunty popped up like a jack-in-the-box—Dodo had never seen her move so fast.

"Granville!"

Dodo frowned. Instead of her usual throaty voice, Bunty had overlaid it with oodles of sugar.

Bunty ran over and enveloped the enormous man in a bear hug so tight that only his square chin was visible. He was clamped against her shoulder, the unkempt eyebrows disappearing under his long fringe in delighted surprise.

The girl dressed in scarlet narrowed her eyes as she watched the pair.

When Bunty put Granville down, he pulled his tweed jacket, straightened his cravat, and placed a possessive arm around her ample shoulders.

"Bunty! It's so good to be here." The phrase was not empty as was so often the case but said with sincerity and true affection. She would have to get the whole story from Bunty later.

19

"Isabella." Bunty bent her knees and kissed the dark-haired girl on both cheeks.

"Hola, señorita."

Spanish.

Bunty grabbed them both by the hand and dragged them over to the fire.

"Let me do the introductions," she said, pushing Isabella onto the couch next to Walter. "Isabella Dominguez, rising star in the opera, meet my cousin, Dodo Dorchester, rising star in the fashion world."

Isabella's face creased into the least sincere smile Dodo had seen since Wilhemina Fanbury told her she liked Dodo's gown at school prize day.

"Delighted!" said Dodo, taking her hand which was limp and cold.

"Granville and I met Isabella during an after-party at the Opera in Bristol, and I just knew I had to invite her to stay," raved Bunty. "I promise you have never heard a voice like hers."

The comparison of the two women was almost comical; Bunty with her horsey, tweed kilt, long socks and sensible shoes, hair sticking everywhere, and Isabella like a stiff, delicate figurine; neat, well-dressed and cold. It baffled the mind.

Isabella sized Dodo up as if they were competing lionesses circling each other before a hunt. Dodo decided to give her a wide berth.

Bunty turned and grabbed her disheveled suitor's arm. "And Granville Post. We met at a cricket match at the end of summer." Her smile had turned as sickly sweet as her tone and she clasped her hands under her chin like some fawning sycophant. Dodo slapped her hand to her mouth to hide a wry smile.

No one could deny that the pair were well matched. They were both unusually tall, in sore need of a refresher course in personal grooming...and clearly infatuated with one another.

Granville grabbed Dodo's hand and clumsily kissed it, keeping his dewy eyes on Bunty.

"Isabella and I traveled down together. I am her sponsor."

"It is lovely to be here Bunty," Isabella said, her accent thick as syrup. "Is it always this cold?" She raised an overplucked eyebrow.

Her thin, satin dress was hardly suitable for a romp on the moors, or a drafty stay at Blackwood. Hopefully, her suitcase held warmer attire.

"Goodness yes! I did warn you," declared Bunty. "We'll have to scrounge up some woolens for you. And this is Walter Montague."

Walter examined Isabella with the same lecherous stare he had bestowed upon Dodo. She returned his impudence with an icy scowl.

"Are you all hungry?" asked Bunty, oblivious to the undercurrent of hostility.

"Rather!" affirmed Granville, his left eye scrunching up in a bizarre type of wink.

Bunty lunged across the room and pulled the bell. "Bread and cheese alright?"

Isabella's lips pulled down into a frown, but Granville's face lit up as though he had just been informed that coq au vin was on the menu. Clearly, Bunty could do no wrong.

As she strode back to rejoin them all at the fire, the door burst open once more and time stood still. Framed in the doorway was a glamorous couple who could have walked straight off the front of a fashion magazine.

Instead of entering, they stood in the doorframe as though inviting the group to applaud them.

Dodo's stomach turned.

Veronica Shufflebottom had arrived.

Dodo froze.

She was sixteen again, on the verge of emerging from puppy fat, oily hair and wide, unruly eyebrows. Memories of her first ball, to which she wore a ghastly emerald dress that her mother had persuaded her into, came thick and fast. Polished, sixteen-year-old Veronica had flounced in that evening wearing a divine creation that simply oozed sophistication and sucked up all the attention.

But that was not enough. Vindictive Veronica had taken the occasion to gather her cronies around her and snicker loudly behind Dodo's back the entire evening. As Dodo swung round the dance floor, virtual knives were thrown into her back from Veronica's cackling brood who spewed their poisonous brew of bitterness. Excessively conscious of her own late development, Dodo's morale had eroded to the point where she had demanded to leave.

The memories flew forward to later that same summer when, trusting her own fashion sense, Dodo had enjoyed a light summer romance with Percy Wallingham until Veronica had swooped in with her talons and hoisted Percy off, only to discard him two days later.

The feud had continued throughout the rest of their school days.

Only now, Dodo reminded herself, *she* was the butterfly, the successful fashion icon emerged from her chrysalis. Veronica had no more power over her.

Dodo narrowed her eyes at the ridiculous spectacle in the doorway.

Still overdramatic.

For the first time she noticed the young man hanging on Veronica's arm.

He must be a fool.

The effect of the couple's appearance on the rest of the party was a shock that numbed them into awed silence.

"Bunty!" cried Veronica in a horrific voice that was reminiscent of squeaky brakes.

Veronica had apparently not yet noticed Dodo who was shielded by Granville as she sat in the corner of the couch closest to the fire.

Dodo stood.

Veronica's glacier-blue eyes bulged in fiery, insolent recognition and her hands tightened around the white fur wrap with a death grip.

"Dodo." She managed to infuse the single word with a thousand insults.

Dodo nodded. "Veronica."

The other occupants in the room stared between the two women as if expecting one of them to draw a gun.

Bunty came to the rescue. "Veronica! You look fabulous. Absolutely smashing! Come in and warm yourself by the fire. It is so drafty in this big, old house. How was your journey?" The nervous words tumbled out without a breath.

Veronica snapped her platinum, marcel-waved head back, giving her full attention to the rest of the people in the room and allowing herself to be conducted to the group around the fire.

"And who is this?" asked Bartie, his arm positioned to shake hands with the exceptionally handsome stranger who had followed Veronica into the room.

"Oh, this is my *boyfriend*, Rupert. Rupert Danforth III." Veronica flashed her white teeth to the room at large as if expecting a prize for having bagged such a fine male specimen. The deer's heads looked on, unimpressed.

Rupert lit up the room with a dazzling smile of his own as he shook Bartie's hand.

In spite of his impeccable wardrobe, Dodo was quick to judge him as shallow and vacuous—what other kind of man would willingly enter a relationship with Veronica Shufflebottom?

"It is simply mar-vel-ous to be here!" Veronica strung out the syllables showering the group with her phony magnanimity. Bile rose in Dodo's throat.

Veronica sank into the old couch and a plume of dust and dog hair rose settling onto the sheen of her sapphire blue dress.

23

The jovial expression that had felt so insincere to Dodo, sagged into an acidic smile as Veronica brushed the dirt off with a white glove.

"Rupert!" Veronica demanded. "Sit here with me!" She patted the couch gently to prevent another flurry of dust.

Rupert's navy eyes hardened almost imperceptibly as he rubbed the back of his neck. "Of course, darling." He folded his firm, athletic frame next to Veronica, and Dodo couldn't help but appreciate the exquisite cut of his oxford bag trousers. Rather than reach for Veronica's hand, he draped his arm along the sofa behind her. The light from the fire caught the refined line of his jaw and square chin.

He flicked his eyes quickly to Dodo—so quickly she thought she might have imagined it.

"Do you know anyone else?" asked Bunty.

Veronica puckered her lips and studied each guest as though they were jewels at Tiffany's.

"I think *I* have had the pleasure," gushed Walter, fondling his weak beard as his eager eyes devoured Veronica. "Walter Montague."

She cut her eyes back to him with no hint of recognition. "You have?"

Walter did not appear in the least fazed that she did not remember him. "It was last year at the regatta in Brighton." He wiggled his nose making his mustache move as though it were a very hairy caterpillar.

Dodo studied Veronica to gauge her response. Walter was neither fashionable nor sophisticated, standards, Dodo seemed to remember, Veronica demanded from her entourage. Her cold eyes flashed.

"Of course." Her smile was flat, and Dodo was convinced that she had no recollection of the forgettable Walter.

Bunty lifted her arm to indicate Granville. "Granville Post, a dear friend of mine from Coventry."

"Delighted," said Veronica, and Rupert bent his lean frame forward to grasp Granville's hand.

"And Isabella Dominguez. Perhaps you have heard of her?" said Bunty.

24

Veronica looked Isabella up and down like the competition for attention that she was.

"No. Sorry should I have?"

Clearly an astute judge of character, Isabella's mouth formed a dangerous grimace. "Unless you are a connoisseur of opera, probably not."

"Opera?" For all Veronica's snobbery, Dodo knew for a fact that in school her tastes and education had not run to the arena of opera.

How will she save face now?

Indecision flashed across Veronica's face. "Yes, well I attend the opera from time to time, but I am soooo busy with other things, charity functions and the like. I'd love to go more often."

Dodo wanted to choke. *Lies.*

Bunty rushed to the rescue. Again.

"Isabella is an up-and-coming soprano. Poised to make her breakthrough in London very soon, I don't doubt."

Isabella's pupils constricted.

"Dominguez?" remarked Rupert, surprising everyone. "Did you perform in Bristol earlier this year?"

An opera buff? Well, well.

The sour expression transformed to a look of utter radiance that shone from Isabella's petite, olive face. "Yes, I did."

"My father saw you and mentioned it. He thoroughly enjoyed your performance." His smooth voice resonated with sincerity which was at odds with his projected persona. Perhaps there was more to this man than met the eye.

Veronica walked her fingers up Rupert's muscular arm. "How very clever of you, darling."

Isabella flipped her luscious curls over her shoulder and rewarded Rupert with a seductive smile that caused Veronica to shift in her seat.

Score one for Isabella.

"That's everyone," said Bartie, pushing his glasses back up his freckled nose. "Nice, intimate little group. What fun we are going to have!"

With Veronica here, I very much doubt it.

Chapter 5

The vast, untamed moors were currently steeped in a dewy mist that clung to the ankles. Dodo was glad Lizzie had packed some rubber boots, though she hated wearing them since they were absolutely hideous. But sometimes function must trump form and today was such a day.

The air was heavy with impending rain and the sky was gray and overcast. Any purple heather was long gone, shriveled to a brown, wet mess. The only beauty was found in the wild ruggedness of the dormant landscape.

Everyone had been spoiled with a late breakfast in bed that morning, and people had been free to pootle around the house until lunch, which had been an enormous meal. As they were all finishing up with coffee, Bunty had announced plans for a ramble on the moors which had been met with a less than enthusiastic reception from almost everyone. Isabella gave the excuse that she had nothing to protect her from the elements, but Bunty had produced an ancient sweater and equally ancient leather boots that were about two sizes too big. Dodo could swear that she recognized them from her youth.

Veronica was no less reluctant, having appeared for lunch in a desperately unsuitable silver, satin dress that hugged her hips and kissed her calves.

"You could have told us last night," she complained to Bunty. "I would have worn something more practical." Rolling her eyes, she had disappeared upstairs and returned in a thick argyle jumper, tartan kilt, and deep brown brogues. Dodo was surprised she owned such serviceable items.

Bunty had rallied everyone with words of encouragement and enthusiasm, and they had all started off as one large group who left the gardens at the back of Blackwood together. However, they had soon clumped into pairs or threesomes with Bartie and Dodo bringing up the rear. Bartie, who was usually bubbling with eagerness, could not quite get his features to agree to a smile. The result was that his dear face was stuck in a kind of hysterical grimace.

"I don't like the moors much anymore," he mumbled, fiddling with glasses that kept steaming up as he leapt large puddles of bog.

"I've noticed. Why is that?" asked Dodo "We used to have such fun as children."

"I took the dogs out a few years ago when a thick fog came down and got stranded in the dark. I can't tell you what terrible noises the moors make at night. The useless dogs had wandered off home leaving me completely alone and I was terrified to move in case I fell in a bog and drowned. You know the moors claim several lives every year."

"Yes," agreed Dodo. "That's one of the reason's your parents were always very strict about us being back by tea-time."

"Exactly! Well, there was nothing to do but stay put and wait it out. I just crouched with my arms round my legs all night and waited for the sun to come up and burn off the fog." He shivered. "I wasn't right for a week. Bad dreams, fever—the works."

"Sounds awful," agreed Dodo. "I'd feel exactly the same if that happened to me. Why didn't you simply stay at the house today?"

"Not very host-like is it? And anyway, Bunty insisted." He pulled the collar of his jacket up to shield his prominent ears from the wind. "She studied the forecast in the paper and promised me there would be no fog today."

"Well, I think it is very brave of you," said Dodo, slipping her arm through her cousin's. "Facing fears is the true definition of courage."

Bartie's mouth curled into a cautious smile. "I'm no hero, Dodo. I'd much rather be by the fire with a hot drink, truth be told. But I wanted to impress Isabella. She's a real corker, isn't she? I was hoping I could partner up with her for the walk, but Walter beat me to it, and we've lost sight of them now." He looked around. "We've lost sight of everyone."

Dodo spun in a circle. "So we have."

They walked on a few paces when Bartie stopped abruptly. "Uggh. Now I have a stone in my shoe." He dropped down to undo the laces with one knee on the ground as he wrestled the shoe off and tipped the offending stone out. When he stood, a large, wet stain showed on his trousers.

"Drat!" He brushed at the fabric trying to sweep the stain away. "Do you think it would be bad form to turn back?"

Dodo looked around again for signs of anyone else, but an infamous moor fog had settled as Bartie had dealt with his shoe. So much for the weather forecast. Bartie turned anxious eyes on her, and the first twinges of worry began to form. She must project confidence for Bartie's sake.

"Not at all. Let's go back together," she declared.

They began to retrace their steps, tiptoeing around mud and divots in the earth, but they had not gone a hundred yards when Dodo noticed that the tall grasses were beginning to disappear from view. The fog was thickening fast. Worry grew like a snowball rolling down a snowy slope.

Bartie was looking down at his feet, watching where he stepped, when Dodo squeezed his arm. "I say!" he complained looking up. "Oh, crikey!" His eyes were wide as soup plates.

"Crikey indeed!" agreed Dodo. "This fog is almost thick enough to taste. How did it happen so fast?" She turned around hoping it was not as dense behind them but could not see more than five feet in either direction.

Bartie gripped her hands. "Perhaps we can call for help?"

They both began shouting but the mist absorbed the sound and bounced it back at them. They listened for a response.

Nothing.

Dodo searched through the gloom, shoving her rising hysteria down deep. It was true that the moors claimed lives.

A strange rasping sound made her stop. Bartie was trembling, his eyes frantic, his breathing short and shallow.

"I say, are you alright?" she asked.

In response, he clapped his hands to his deathly white face, unable to speak. She had never seen her cousin like this. Taking control of the situation she placed her hands on his shoulders and pressed down.

"Take deep breaths, Bartie," she said calmly. "In and out, in and out."

With effort, he slowly regained command of his breathing. "It's happening all over again," he moaned.

"Nonsense, you are not alone, and we have at least an hour before it starts to get dark. Come on!"

Feigning a confidence she did not feel, Dodo moved forward, pulling Bartie behind her, watching every step carefully and praying that they were headed in the right direction. She continued to hope that they might bump into some of the others.

They picked their way along as the oppressive fog distilled on her hair and clothes leaving her soaked through. As the temperature dropped, her muscles began to tremble in uncontrollable shivers and the snarl of concern in her stomach was now the size of a football. The moors were a dangerous opponent, and she silently cursed the weathermen who had assured an unsuspecting public that they posed no threat today.

Bartie had shrunk in on himself, and she felt as though she was towing a small schoolboy rather than a grown man—but she could not blame him. The trauma he was experiencing was real and all-consuming.

Rising to the challenge of protector, adrenaline surged as her survival instinct kicked in to gear. She was blowed if she was going to die out here on the moors! On and on they advanced, one careful step at a time.

As Dodo's foot thrust forward once more, the ground vanished and she sank forward into an unstable, sticky goo that swallowed her boot and trickled over the top and into her woolen socks.

A bog has bitten!

"Ahhh!" she cried out.

Bartie froze.

The thick, brown swamp sucked her foot with unexpected force, and she slipped her hand round and grabbed Bartie's wrist.

"I'm stuck," she wailed.

"Stay calm. No need to panic." Bartie's voice sounded strong and capable. It was if the emergency had jolted him out of his own fear. She felt him pull on her wrist with great strength.

"It's like quicksand!" shouted Dodo as her foot sank farther.

29

Bartie braced himself, bending both knees, and pulled as if her life depended on it. Her foot did not budge. Filthy mud was fast filling the rubber boot.

"Anything?" asked Bartie.

"Not yet. Let me change my grip." She put both hands around his wrist and as he lunged low, her foot slithered out of the boot that remained stuck in the bog and she fell, exhausted, onto the wet earth.

"Bother!"

"Oh dear!" exclaimed Bartie, staring at her sodden, stockinged foot. "Now we are both dirty as well as wet. Do you want to try and get it?" He was peering into the wretched marsh.

"No. Far too dangerous," she replied. "Let's just keep going."

Limping along behind Bartie, who had now taken the lead, sharp stones dug into her foot and just as she despaired of ever getting back safely, Bartie declared, "I think we've made it!"

The dark, imposing shadow of Blackwood loomed in front of them and had never looked so comforting. "Oh, thank heavens!"

For fear of encountering more bogs, they continued inching forward until they broke free of the moors and were safely back on the lawn.

Running, they pushed through the back door and into the welcoming light of the house and right into Lizzie.

"Oh!" yelled the maid, rushing to give her mistress a quick hug. "I've been so worried. That fog came down something awful and …" She stopped and stared at Dodo's foot.

"I lost a boot in the bog."

"Oh m'lady. You could have been drowned!"

"Not at all. Bartie rescued me."

Her cousin bristled with pride.

"Here, have a seat and I will get you both some tea," said Lizzie.

"I'm going up to change and go in search of something stronger," announced Bartie and banged through the door to the main house.

Lizzie brought the tea and Dodo drank in great, unladylike gulps. Lizzie's eyes widened and she hid a smile behind her hand.

"Don't look at me like that, Lizzie. I am in a state of distress. You are right. I didn't like to mention it while Bartie was here, but we could have died out there." The smile slipped from Lizzie's face like butter off the edge of warm toast.

"I'm sorry m'lady. It's just I'm not used to seeing you drink tea like my dad."

"Yes, well. A brush with death changes a person."

Lizzie raised one eyebrow.

"I'm being a little dramatic, but it was a sticky situation. Bartie was no help at first as he had been traumatized years ago by a similar incident involving a night spent on the moors alone. But he rose to the occasion in the end." Dodo drained the last of the tea. "Who else is back?"

"No one. The cook has been chewing her nails since the fog came down. So many people out there who aren't familiar with the moors. She's pacing all over like a hungry bear."

The tangle of worry returned.

The back door blew open. A windswept Bunty fell through, closely followed by a dripping Granville. He reached behind him to help a wild-eyed Isabella, whose soggy curls were trembling.

"Dodo!" cried Bunty. "I am so glad you are back. Have you seen Bartie?" Her skin was strained over her jaw as she clenched her teeth.

"Yes!" Dodo reassured her. "We came back together."

Anxiety drained from Bunty's face like dirty water from a bathtub. "I have been so worried!" Her brow squished into a question and she lowered her voice. "Is he...alright?"

"He's doing better now. You should have warned me he was terrified of the moors."

"I swear to you, the forecast did not call for fog or I would never have agreed to Walter's suggestion of a walk. 'Overcast skies' was all it said."

"Your weatherman should be fired," stuttered Isabella, black mascara dripping down her cheeks from the humidity. Her sweater was soaked, and mud splattered her legs, which were revealed as she bent to peel off the borrowed boots.

"If I never go rambling again it will be too soon," she complained, rolling the 'r' dramatically and shivering violently.

31

"And if I come down with a cold, my agent will be furious. I have a performance next week."

Bunty's fingers were pressed together, her knuckles moving up and down rapidly. "I feel so responsible," she groaned.

Granville slapped her across the back. "Not your fault, old thing," he began, his eyebrows wiggling around. "You couldn't have known, and we are back safe and sound."

"But where are the others? Are Veronica, Rupert and Walter in the drawing room?" she asked.

"No one else is back," said Dodo quietly, a chill creeping over her.

"What? No one?" Bunty's face fell.

"I am sure they will be here soon," replied Dodo, though she was having doubts. She may not like Veronica, but she did not wish her lost on the moors.

Isabella was wiping her face, smearing the mascara farther. Dodo handed her a towel that was hanging on a hook.

"Here, you have some"—she circled her own face with a finger—"on your face."

Isabella rushed to the window to inspect the damage, wiping furiously. Then she wrapped the towel around her wet curls. "English weather! It is not my favorite."

"Quite so, quite so," said Granville to no one in particular.

Worry was now etched all over Bunty's features. "As soon as the fog fell, I cried out, but no one responded. I know the moors like the back of my hand, but even I lost my way a little." She bit one of her nails. "I do hope they're alright!" She peered through the dark window, but the swirling fog made visibility impossible.

"Ohhh!" she groaned.

Granville put a clumsy arm around her, and she buried her wet face in his equally wet jacket.

"Well, I am going up to soak in the bath," declared Isabella and padded her way out of the room.

Lizzie had been very quiet, absorbing all the nervous energy. Dodo caught her eye and tipped her head. Lizzie took the hint and left the room.

"Try not to give in to hopelessness," Dodo began, attempting to soothe her cousin though the knot in her own stomach was growing exponentially. "Don't think the worst—"

A loud thud at the door startled everyone in the mudroom. The handle turned, and two dark figures pushed into the light.

"That was without a doubt, the worst activity ever!" shrieked Veronica. "Whose bally idea was that? Are you trying to kill us?"

"Calm down, Veronica. We're safe now." The deep furrows on Rupert's brow betrayed his irritation. Perhaps cracks were forming in their relationship? His jacket was around Veronica's shoulder and his damp shirt was clinging to his chest. Dodo looked away.

"Calm down! Calm down! I will not calm down." Veronica pointed a finger at Bunty. "She is trying to murder us. I've a good mind to leave right now." Her platinum blond Marcel waves were no more, the white hair hanging in rats' tails. And her sensible shoes were caked in dry mud. The vestiges of her sophistication were somewhere out on the moors.

"Uh, the fog is too thick to go anywhere," Rupert pointed out.

"Ohhh!" Veronica slapped her hand on the wall. "I have never been so frightened." As the last word escaped, she slumped forward.

Dodo fancied that she was being theatrical, but Rupert sprang to her side. "She's in a faint," he declared. "I shall take her to her room, and I expect brandy to be brought right away."

Who is he to order Bunty around?

"Of course. I'll see to it right away," Bunty replied meekly.

Rupert scooped Veronica into his arms as if she weighed no more than a blanket. She lay limp and listless, her head hanging back like an actress in a silent film.

Dodo chewed her lip.

Granville followed Rupert to the door and opened it.

"I am so relieved they are back safely but what a disaster!" cried Bunty, sinking to a bench that sat along the wall. "I'm beginning to wish we had never hosted this stupid party."

Dodo reached out and put her hand over Bunty's. "Don't pay any attention to Veronica. She is a negative ninny and would complain about the least little thing. She's not a very nice person at the best of times."

Bunty looked up, her eyes pulled together tight as if she was trying not to cry.

"And you cannot control the weather, Bunty. This is not your fault. We are just a bunch of spoiled socialites. We'll get over it."

"I hope so," Bunty said, looking forlorn.

Dodo started to shiver again. "I'm going to have a bath too. Coming?"

"No. I want to wait for Walter to return. He's the last one. I won't be able to rest until he is safely back. Will you see to the brandy?"

"Of course," said Dodo. "Would you like some company while you wait?"

"No, I'm fine." Looking like an abandoned puppy, Bunty reached for Granville's hand. "Go and have a warm bath."

Dodo was really getting very cold and knew that Lizzie would have drawn her a bath by now.

"If you are sure?"

"I'm sure."

She looked anything but.

Chapter 6

Wrapped in a pure silk kimono with fluffy slippers, her hair wrapped up in a towel, Dodo collapsed into a chair as she took a sip of hot milk.

"Lizzie this is just what I needed," she declared. Looking at her maid, she noticed that her eyebrows were forming a deep 'v'. "Whatever is the matter?"

Lizzie sucked in her lips. "Mr. Montague has still not returned."

A glance at the clock told Dodo that over two hours had passed since her own return.

"Oh! That cannot be good." The sky outside the windows was dark, and still dense with fog.

She put the mug of milk down. "How is Bunty?"

Lizzie crossed her arms. "Nervy, like my Auntie Lil."

As Dodo grimaced there was a sharp knock at her bedroom door.

"Come in!" she called.

Bunty's large, curly head peeked in. "Oh, you *are* out of the bath. Can we talk?"

"Of course. Lizzie, would you be a dear and fetch me some toast?"

The two women changed places as Lizzie slipped out and Bunty stalked in and sat down heavily on the bed, pushing her hair back so hard that her eyes stretched up.

"Walter's not back," she groaned, running the hands down her long face. "What shall we do?"

One of Bunty's socks was hanging around her ankle and there was a tea stain on her blouse. If the circumstances were less dire, Dodo would wrangle her cousin into deportment and grooming lessons. Lack of attention to appearance was one thing when you were a child but quite another when you were a grown woman. But now was not the time and Dodo averted her eyes from the regrettable sock.

"Oh, that is unfortunate."

"It's more than unfortunate, Dodo. The temperature is supposed to drop tonight posing the added danger of exposure. I feel just awful. Should we call the police or something?"

Dodo came to sit beside her cousin. "I don't believe anyone would be able to get through from the village in this fog. It's thick as treacle. But I would be happy to go out on the lawn with electric torches and shout? If he happened to be close, he could follow our voices."

Bunty's eyes brightened. "Would you? I feel that I must do something, and I don't want to bother Granville with it all."

"Of course," said Dodo shaking the towel from her head. "Let me change and dry my hair."

Ten minutes later, wearing a thick, skull cap and a Fair Isle jumper with borrowed boots, Dodo was waving a torch around and yelling at the top of her voice where the lawn met the moors. Hardly even able to see Bunty, whose considerable shadow in the fog brought to mind a gothic monster, dread of failure washed over Dodo. The uselessness of their actions was obvious. No one would be able to find their way back in this.

Walter was lost for the night…or worse.

After shouting for thirty minutes, they were both hoarse and Dodo called a halt to the proceedings.

"We cannot keep this up all night, Bunty. He is a grown man and has hopefully found some shelter where he can stay put till morning. If he is not back by tomorrow, I will come with you to find him at first light."

"I hope you are right," Bunty said with little confidence.
Me too.

§

Dodo was dreaming of peach chiffon ball gowns when the beautiful girls on the catwalk stopped and turned toward a knocking sound. The girls vanished in a puff of smoke and Dodo realized that the knocking was real.

She rolled out of bed and opened her door to find Bunty, eyes blood shot, wearing the same clothes as the day before. Dawn was barely beginning.

"Bunty, you look bally awful!"

"I haven't slept a wink all night." she admitted, pulling out a man's handkerchief and blowing her nose solidly. "Are you ready?"

The clock said it was seven, but it felt more like four in the morning to Dodo.

She indicated her red silk pajamas. "Not really."

"Well, hurry then. I can't rest till we find him." Bunty's red nose was quivering with nerves, touching Dodo's compassion.

She slipped into the trousers she had worn the evening before and a thick cardigan, with a scarf and coat. She pulled a woolen beret over her black bob, and the two women tiptoed through the quiet house and out to the lawn. It was still pretty foggy, though the increasing daylight helped, and Dodo could see as much as ten feet ahead. Her stomach gurgled but food would have to wait.

"I brought some orange yarn," said Bunty as she plunged into the garden. "That way we can find our way back. I would have brought red, but I couldn't find it."

"Jolly good idea, Bunty."

"I'll tie it to that tree." She pointed to a large oak on the edge of the property. "I'll unwind it as we go."

It was significantly colder than the previous day, and Dodo pulled the beret down over her ears. Bunty's stride was so long and hurried that Dodo had to run to keep up with her.

So much for a lazy week away.

After Bunty secured the yarn she forged ahead, and Dodo followed in her wake. The borrowed galoshes were a trifle big and she could already feel a blister forming.

When they got a little deeper into the moors, Bunty slowed. "I think we should keep a sharp eye out and perhaps call again."

Dodo winced. Her throat had not quite recovered from the day before. "Will do."

They both cried Walter's name but the only response was silence.

Bunty plunged on again and repeated the routine several more times. Dodo was beginning to feel that it was another exercise in futility.

When the ball of yarn ran out, Bunty stopped to tie a
second skein to the first and Dodo looked around. Just a few feet
ahead she could see a drop. She walked over and found a twenty-
foot chasm with a nasty bog at its base. Her foot clipped a tuft of
long grass and something dark moved, startling her. She dropped
down to see what it was.

A black felt hat.

"I say Bunty, come here."

Bunty looked up from the yarn, her eyes fixing on the hat.
"Golly. That looks a lot like the hat Walter was wearing
yesterday." She padded across the peaty ground and took a look
over the edge.

The fog was settling at the bottom of the drop but swirling
in the mild breeze.

"Look, there! What do you think that is?" Bunty cried.

As the fog parted slightly, a flash of red appeared. "I think
it's a scarf," said Dodo, an ominous feeling effervescing inside her.

"Great Scott!" screamed Bunty, her skin as white as the
fog. "Walter must have fallen over the edge." Her hand flew to her
throat. "Do you think...could he..." The sentence hung unfinished.

Dodo crouched by the edge of the cliff, searching with her
hands. The long grass was flattened by the edge of the drop. She
indicated it to Bunty.

"Dash it all!" Bunty cried. "The reason Walter didn't come
back is because he's dead!"

Chapter 7

The fog was thickening again as they followed the orange yarn back to Blackwood. Little was said as Dodo left Bunty to embrace her shock while she considered her options.

The truth was that it was unlikely that Walter was still alive if he had, indeed, fallen into the marshy water, since he had not responded to their cries. Now that things were more certain, Dodo felt an urgent need to alert the local police to the situation, even if the fog was too thick for them to reach the house at present. She had a responsibility to initiate the investigative process so that as soon as the fog lifted, they could come to retrieve the body.

An alternative line of thinking, that Walter might still be alive but unable to respond for some reason, sat around her shoulders like Jacob Marley's chain.

Once they reached the house, Dodo asked Mrs. Brown to make Bunty a sweet cup of tea and ordered her to drink it, while she went in search of the ancient Blackwood telephone.

Dodo's late uncle had been an amateur scientist who dabbled in telegraphy and early telephones. The one in current use at Blackwood dated from the late 1800's and was an unwieldy beast. The transmitter was powered by a local battery which was cranked by a handle. In the past, these batteries were checked by the telephone companies but since modern telephones used electricity from the same wires that carried the voice signals, it was a technology that was no longer supported by them. If no one in the house had remembered to replace the battery, the phone could be completely dead however much one cranked it.

Another outdated and inconvenient problem with the contraption was that it only had one portal, which was bally inconvenient as you had to use the same port to listen and to speak. The Gillingsworth's penchant for written communication and a certain nostalgia for the decrepit machine, meant that Bartie had no interest in updating his equipment.

The old, square apparatus stood on an even older spindly table under the servant's stairs. She turned the hand generator and held her breath. Lifting the telephone to her ear she heard an encouraging crackle.

"Operator!" The quality of the prim voice was almost as rough as the line.

"Police!" cried Dodo, hurrying in case the line failed.

"Nature of the problem?"

"A possible dead body."

The voice at the other end seemed to forget all decorum.

"Dead body?" the operator gasped in shock. "Oh, my goodness! Are you alright?"

Dodo's lip hitched up. "I'm fine. There has been an accident. Please put me through to the police."

"I'm forgetting myself," apologized the old lady. "Putting you through."

"Tarnstable Police Station. Constable Barrow speaking. How may I help you?" This voice was middle-aged, and Dodo imagined a portly gentleman with a thatch of graying hair.

"I'm calling from Blackwood House. There has been an accident on the moors. We believe someone may have died from a fall."

"Believe?"

"We found a hat on the edge of a sharp drop and saw a scarf in the bog below early this morning, after the man in question went missing from a ramble yesterday."

"To whom am I speaking?"

"Lady Dorothea Dorchester, cousin of Lord Gillingsworth."

"I'll send someone out immediately, m'lady. Be on the lookout."

"Thank you, consta—" The line went dead.

Drat!

Dodo returned to the kitchen to report, just in time to see Bunty pouring a generous amount of whiskey into her tea.

"Bunty! It's not even nine o' clock!"

"I know," she said with a burp, indicating that this dose was a refill. "I just can't..."

"This is no time to go all wobbly on me, darling. The police are on their way."

Bunty tipped her chin down and looked at Dodo through her unruly locks.

"I feel so responsible. *I* made everyone go on the walk."

"Don't be silly. You cannot blame yourself." She turned to the cook. "Mrs. Brown, please make Bunty some scrambled eggs. The last thing I need is a drunk woman on my hands at a time like this. Let's sober her up." Dodo swept the whiskey bottle away.

"Of course, m'lady."

Dodo glanced at the kitchen clock, leaving Bunty in the charge of the cook and went in search of Lizzie. She needed to talk to someone sensible and sober.

She went to her room and found Lizzie getting an outfit ready for the day.

"M'lady!" said Lizzie face white with shock, dropping the skirt she was holding. "Where have you been?"

Dodo pulled off the beret and smoothed her hair. "On the moors." She sunk onto the bed and pulled the covers around her. She felt suddenly chilled to the bone.

"The moors at this hour?"

"Mr. Montague did not return last night." Her teeth were beginning to chatter. She wasn't sure if it was shock or the cold.

Lizzie sat on the bed next to her mistress. "I did wonder," she said. "He didn't bring a valet, so no one knew anything at breakfast."

"It will be all over the house in no time. I've called the police. They should be here within the hour."

Lizzie turned her head to look out the window. Dodo followed suit. All they could see was thick, white mist. The fog had returned with a vengeance.

Lizzie turned back. "I don't think they will be able to make it out here in this weather."

"I hope you are wrong," sighed Dodo.

"Shall I bring some breakfast up, m'lady? You look done in."

"Would you be a dear?"

Lizzie hurried downstairs and Dodo slid under the covers trying to bring her body temperature back up. She must have

41

dropped off to sleep as she roused when Lizzie returned with a tray.

"I just brought some porridge and tea. After the shock you've had you probably won't feel up to anything else."

Dodo managed a sleepy smile. "What would I do without you, Lizzie?"

A wry grin spread over Lizzie's face. "I often ask myself the same question, m'lady."

"If I wasn't so tired, I would become indignant at your tone," said Dodo reaching for the tray.

Lizzie placed it on the eiderdown and plumped up the pillows. "I shouldn't be so flippant given the circumstances," said Lizzie. "Every time I look out the window at that fog it gives me the shivers." She covered her mouth with her hand and shook her head. "Poor man."

She picked up some leather shoes. "I'll leave you to eat while I polish these and see what the scuttlebutt is downstairs. I'll come back to help you dress."

"Jolly good." Dodo sat and picked up the warm teacup. "And make sure Bunty doesn't get hold of the whiskey again."

"Again?" asked Lizzie as she headed for the door.

Dodo dipped her chin and stared at her maid. "Long story."

The porridge was warm and sticky and just what she needed. When she had finished, she checked the time. The police should be here by now. Warm and full, weariness attacked, and she snuggled back under the covers.

When Lizzie returned, Dodo guiltily dragged herself back to a conscious state.

"What are they saying?" she murmured.

"Well, one of the house maids is frightening herself with tall tales about werewolves and ghosts attacking people at night on the moors. Mrs. Brown had to put a stop to that. And the maid who was assigned to Mr. Montague's room went to check and the bed has not been slept in. It does not look good."

"The moors are like a monster, eating victims every year," Dodo said. "If that blasted weatherman had got his forecast right, we would never have gone for a walk."

42

Lizzie picked up a mother of pearl hairbrush and stroked it through Dodo's hair.

"How is Bunty?" Dodo asked.

Lizzie laid down the brush. "Mrs. Brown has hustled her out of the kitchen to sleep it off."

"That's probably just as well with the police coming. Bartie will be no good as he was not with us, so I suppose it will fall to me to talk to the police."

"Well, you do have experience with this kind of thing," commented Lizzie as she dragged a wet comb through Dodo's hair and used the new hairdryer to style the bob. "Murder and intrigue seem to follow wherever you go."

"Yes, but this is not murder," corrected Dodo. "I have experience with that. Not accidents."

§

Dressed in a navy wool skirt, cream woolen tights, and an ivory cashmere sweater, Dodo sat in the drawing room fiddling with her string of pearls while waiting for everyone to gather after elevenses.

The first to enter was Isabella. Clearly unprepared for British weather in November, she smoothed her lilac chiffon dress as she sat as close to the fire as possible.

Rather than repeat the sordid story numerous times, Dodo filled the gap with small talk. In spite of their rocky start, Isabella proved to be an intelligent girl who spoke excellent English but complained about the weather more than was polite.

Granville was next. He had combed his long hair back which was a great improvement, but his large mustache was still horribly untidy. He loped across the room and bent his angular frame onto the couch farthest from the fireplace.

"I say, have you seen Bunty this morning?" he asked.

"Yes. She's around somewhere." Dodo waved a hand, leaving her statement vague.

She was saved from further deception by the arrival of Bartie who was looking rather chipper. It was a shame she was

43

going to have to spoil his good mood. He sat uncomfortably close to Isabella who hugged the arm of the sofa even more.

"Still foggy," he said, unnecessarily.

"I hope it won't stay like this for the whole weekend," complained Isabella. "I shall die of cold."

"Here," said Bartie, putting an arm around her shoulder. "I can keep you warm."

Isabella picked up his arm as though it were a snake and placed it back in his lap. "That is too kind of you."

Bertie's whole face collapsed as her rejection punctured his good mood like a nail in a tire.

Veronica and Rupert walked in, arm in arm, completing the group. Veronica was dressed in ruby red, wide-legged trousers, and a polka-dotted black and white blouse paired with a pink cardigan.

Dodo wrinkled her nose. *Pink with red?*

"Darlings! What's on the agenda today?" Veronica had obviously recovered her spirits from yesterday.

"Actually," began Dodo. "There has been a change of plans." Every eye in the room settled on her. "I'm sorry to have to tell you that Walter did not return from the moors last night and…is presumed dead."

Veronica gasped, her large, red lips open wide, and Isabella and Granville cried out together, "What?"

"How do you know?" asked Rupert, his tone calm and even.

"Bunty was up all night, waiting for his return. When he was not back early this morning, she woke me, and we went on a rescue mission."

"In this fog?" asked Rupert.

Was that a hint of concern in his voice?

"It was not so thick at seven this morning," she explained. "We found his hat at the top of a drop-off, and his red scarf was floating in a marshy pond at the bottom."

"Oh! How terrible," said Isabella.

Bartie was white as a sheet.

"I've called the police," Dodo continued. "I hope they will arrive any minute."

"I don't think so," contradicted Granville, pulling his hand down his mustache. "No way anyone could drive safely in these conditions."

Rupert disentangled his arm from Veronica and went to look out of the French windows that were partially covered with thick curtains. He pulled them back, revealing a thick veil of mist.

"Granville is right," he agreed. "No one is coming here today."

Chapter 8

The ever-thickening fog was a problem. Blackwood House sat on the edge of the moors in the worst of the swirling mist. But Dodo hoped the police would have called back if they were unable to reach them. Perhaps it was time to call again.

Leaving everyone else muttering in the drawing room, Dodo hurried back to the phone and cranked the handle on the box. On this occasion when she lifted the contraption to her ear there was no crackle.

"Hello! Hello!" she called.

Nothing.

They were alone. She replaced the telephone, cursing that neither Uncle Matthew nor Bartie had ever updated it and exhaled in exasperation.

However, this was not a murder investigation. As far as she could tell it was simply a tragic accident, but the thought that things would be unresolved until the dense fog lifted was still unnerving. And the awful situation would be a crushing dampener on the group since it would be totally irreverent to laugh and have fun while one of their number was floating in a bog. Plus, she felt the weight of responsibility to alert his next of kin, which was clearly impossible in these conditions.

She walked slowly back to the rest of the group rehearsing what she would say.

As she pushed open the door the low-level murmuring stopped. She walked over to the fireplace and stood facing everyone.

"The telephone is not working and with the fog like this, Granville is right. The police will not be able to come. But we can stay calm. We are all adults and there is no evidence of foul play—"

A dry cough from Isabella interrupted her narrative.

"Did you have something to say, Isabella?"

The Spanish opera singer puckered her lips and narrowed her eyes. "May I speak to you in private?"

A shift in mood crept through the room, gazes swinging round like spotlights in a prison yard.

Dodo put her hands in her pockets as worry gnawed at the unexpected request. "Of course. Why don't we go to the library?"

The babble resumed.

Dodo led Isabella to the old library. As usual the room smelled faintly of mildew and mold. She approached the desk under which she had spent many happy hours as a child reading Moby Dick and Treasure Island and motioned for Isabella to sit on one of the worn leather chairs.

"You do not believe this is an accident?" Dodo began.

"I do not know," started the small girl, with worried eyes. "But the night we arrived I heard an argument in the foyer which is just below my room. Curious, I tiptoed out to see who it was, keeping myself hidden in the shadows. It was the chap who is with that hussy Veronica, and Walter."

Dodo bit back a smile. "Rupert? Did you hear what they were fighting about?"

"I could not hear everything. Their voices were fierce but low. I did hear the words, 'insult' and 'unchivalrous' and then Rupert got very close to Walter's face and sneered, saying something I could not hear. Then Rupert ran up the stairs and I hurried back to my room."

"So, you think Rupert may have been angry enough to push Walter off the cliff?" This was information she had not anticipated. Rupert's intelligence may be up for debate, but he did not appear in the least violent.

"I am not saying that. No. But you said there was no foul play involved. But this is important, no? A man argues with another man and he ends up drowned in a bog."

Dodo pursed her lips. She considered the lean, debonair man with the startling blue eyes. Could he be a cold-blooded killer? Whatever her opinion on the matter, Isabella's testimony did change the dynamics.

What were the two men fighting about? Did Rupert know Walter? They had appeared to be strangers but perhaps they were not. Time to put on her detective hat, it seemed. And this time there would be no help from the police.

47

She crossed her ankles. "Who were you with on the walk when the fog came down?"

Isabella's eyes flicked up to the ceiling. "I started off with Bunty, Veronica, Walter, Granville and Rupert but we hadn't got far when I had trouble with my shoes—they were too big, and my sock had slid down under my arch. It was extremely uncomfortable, and I stopped to pull it back up so that it didn't give me a blister. Bunty and Granville stayed with me. Walter, Veronica and Rupert carried on and got swallowed up in the fog. We could not see them anymore. We called out to them but got no response. They must have been quite far ahead at that point."

"Was that the last time you saw them on the moors?"

"Yes. We continued for a while but as the fog became worse Bunty got nervous and decided we should return. She cried out again, but no one responded, and we made our way back. It was frightening and I was glad to be with Bunty who knows the way, as we could not see more than a few feet ahead."

"There are plenty of dangers on the moors. I got stuck in a bog and lost my boot!" said Dodo.

Isabella wrapped her arms around her body. "This place is not very nice. I shall be glad to go home."

"Don't judge it too harshly," warned Dodo. "When the weather is good, Blackwood is paradise. I have many happy memories here."

"If you say so. I'm not made for this kind of weather or terrain." Isabella shivered.

Dodo stood. "Thank you, Isabella. I do have some experience with investigations, and I think your testimony warrants one. Did you know anyone other than Bunty and Granville before arriving?"

"No. I am here at the invitation of Bunty. She is odd but I like her. One does not have to pretend around her."

"I know exactly what you mean," agreed Dodo.

"In my line of work there is a great deal of pretension," said Isabella. "It can be exhausting. I came to Blackwood to relax and get away from all of that." Dodo flashed back to the vision of Isabella with wet hair and cheeks smudged with black mascara. She had looked vulnerable then. Today she was all put together, but she was far from relaxed, anxiety peeking out from behind her eyes.

"I can well imagine. I came here to get away from it all too— but for different reasons."

Isabella quirked a finely plucked brow.

"Trouble in the romance department," Dodo clarified.

"Ah! Say no more. I completely understand." Isabella stood and they went back to the warm drawing room.

Veronica jumped up pointing a finger at Isabella. "What did she say? I think we have a right to know! Is she accusing someone of something?"

"Calm down, Veronica." Dodo's voice was firm and authoritative.

"Calm down!" she screeched. "Why do people keep saying that to me?"

Because you are a temperamental brat.

Arms crossed and features hard, Veronica screamed, "I demand to know what she said!"

"Why? Do you have something to hide, Veronica?" Dodo arranged her features into a sweet smile.

"No, of course not!" Veronica flapped her arms. "But that doesn't stop people making baseless accusations."

And you would know.

Returning to the fireplace so that she could see everyone, Dodo clasped her hands behind her back.

"I *will* say that Isabella's statement does necessitate some follow up. It is certainly not definitive, but I think we owe it to Walter to investigate a little to ensure that this was just an unfortunate accident." She cast an eye at Rupert. Instead of reclining he was sitting bolt upright sending furtive glances in Isabella's direction.

"Surely, we'll have to wait for the police and who knows when they will get here?" he asked, dragging his hand across his mouth.

"Actually," began Bartie. "My cousin has quite the reputation as an amateur detective. I propose that we allow her to start the investigation."

49

"Absolutely not!" howled Veronica. "She has no authority here."

"On the contrary," Bartie said. "As the owner of this establishment, if I ask her to begin an investigation, that invests her with the authority. Does it not?"

Everyone began to talk at once until Bartie clapped his hands. "How about we put it to a vote?"

At that very moment, Bunty entered the room looking worse for wear, her hair awry and her tired eyes fixed to the floor. A slight wince suggested a hangover headache. Granville reached for her and she snuggled under his arm.

"What's all the fuss?" she asked, eyes bleary.

"Bartie has suggested that Dodo begin an investigation," explained Isabella.

"Why?" Bunty's face creased with confusion. "It was an accident. Wasn't it?"

"I very much hope so," said Dodo. "But someone witnessed something that may lead in another direction."

Bunty slapped her chest. "What? No!"

"Yes. I think old Walter deserves us to look into it, don't you?" asked Bartie.

Bunty's features telegraphed that she did not think so, but she gave a reluctant nod.

"And I proposed that Dodo do the investigating since the police can't get here, what with her reputation and everything."

Bunty turned to Dodo. "Oh yes! She *is* good at this sort of thing. She has worked with Scotland Yard on more than one occasion."

"Really?" said Veronica and Rupert in unison.

"Yes. Now, let's put it to the vote." Bartie looked around the room brows raised. "Those in favor?"

Isabella, Bunty, Bartie and Granville immediately assented with raised hands.

Veronica could not have looked more sour if she were sucking on a lemon, and kept her hands firmly on her knees. Rupert seemed less sure, but after a poison look from Veronica, remained in concert with his girlfriend.

"We just need a majority," said Bartie, "which we have."

50

"This is ridiculous!" blustered Veronica and stalked from the room. "Rupert!"

A variety of expressions passed over Rupert's face as he looked from person to person avoiding Dodo's eye completely. *Was he guilty?* He rose slowly and followed Veronica, stopping once as if to speak but then thinking better of it.

"What dreadful manners!" hissed Bunty when the door closed.

"What do you need us to do?" Bartie asked Dodo.

"A private word with everyone is the first order of business," explained Dodo. "I'll start with Bunty if that's alright. Give Veronica time to cool off. Are you up for tea in your room, Bunty?"

She tipped her head back as if it weighed a ton. "I suppose so. This weekend just goes from bad to worse," she muttered. "Let's get it over with."

"Stiff upper lip, old girl," said Granville.

Chapter 9

Bunty's childhood bedroom was the perfect example of function over form. Never one to be interested in pink or frilly things, her bedding was plain blue as were the curtains. It was a large room with a bank of windows overlooking the gardens and the moors beyond. One side of the room was set up as a sitting area with mis-matched chairs around a fireplace. Dodo settled herself on one side inviting the distracted Bunty to sit on the other.

"Why the investigation? Is it really necessary?" Bunty was clearly having second thoughts.

Dodo nodded. "I'm afraid it is. Isabella told me something that calls into question the 'unfortunate accident' theory."

"Can you tell me what she said?" Bunty's eyes were pleading.

"Not yet," responded Dodo. "I want to keep it confidential and then see if anyone else corroborates her statement."

Bunty rested her cheek on her shoulder so that her eye squashed closed, a habit from childhood. "That makes sense, I suppose."

"First, I need to know about everyone here. Why you invited them, what you know about them— that kind of thing. Let's start with Veronica. You said she never mentioned that we went to school together?"

Bunty's mouth twisted. "No."

"Which makes me wonder what she is up to. How did the invitation come about?"

"It was sort of last minute, actually. I was at a late game of polo last week with some friends and Veronica happened to be in the seat next to me. Rupert was one of the players and she was not shy in singing his praises. It's always more interesting if you know a player, so I kept my eye on him and she and I got to chatting. She asked me where I lived and about myself and I couldn't help it, Dodo, but I boasted about being your cousin—you are a bit of a celebrity you know—and I am so very dull and Veronica is...well, you know, and I felt the need to embellish my resumé. Veronica became very interested—perhaps that should have tipped me off.

Anyway, I told her that I was having a low-key weekend party and that you were coming and…now that I think about it, she kind of invited herself."

Dodo narrowed her eyes. "So, she and Rupert were an item?"

"Seemed to be. Yes, else why would she be there with him? My friends were in a hurry to get something to eat and we left before the match ended so I didn't see them together."

Dodo tapped her pencil on her notebook. "What did she tell you about herself?"

"Not much now that you come to mention it. She gave some song and dance about being in the inner circle of the royals—"

Dodo choked on her tea. "That is an outright lie. Her father isn't even a peer."

"Well, that's what she told me. She also claimed to be a world traveler and an authority on fashion—"

"Have you noticed her outfits?" said Dodo, barking out a stiff laugh. "What am I saying, of course you haven't? You have no interest in the art of dressing but take it from me she is a pretender."

"I daresay you are right."

Dodo leaned forward to place her empty cup on the table. "Can you remember anything else?"

"She did a lot of name dropping, but then so had I, so who was I to judge?" Her face folded into a guilty frown.

"That sounds about right. Veronica is a thoroughly nasty piece of work. No doubt her plans involve humiliating me in some way."

Bunty spread her hands. "Perhaps she's jealous and wants to show you she has achieved things too."

Dodo narrowed her eyes and murmured. "She's up to something." She doodled while she thought. "What about Rupert?"

"Didn't meet him before this weekend. Veronica did tell me he's in line for a title. Can't remember what it is."

"Hence her interest in him." Dodo made a note. "She always was desperate to climb the social ladder. I'm beginning to feel sorry for the horrible man."

"Rupert? Has he acted badly toward you?"

Dodo dropped her chin. "Not really. But anyone who's interested in the likes of Veronica must be below average intelligence."

Bunty crossed her long legs, hands clasped around her bulky skirt. "So, you've not noticed his film star looks?" Her words were laced with sarcasm.

Dodo snapped her eyes up to Bunty's. She was unused to her cousin noticing the opposite sex.

"I may not be a beauty like you, Dodo, but I'm not blind." Bunty had forgotten the tragedy for a moment and was grinning from ear to ear. "Even I can see that he is a dazzlingly handsome man."

Dodo chuckled.

Putting aside his egregious character flaw, she reflected on Rupert's classic features and striking appearance. "I may have noticed," she admitted. "But his relationship with Veronica disqualified him from further attention. He obviously has no common sense."

Bunty rubbed the threadbare arm of her chair. "I'm not sure he really likes her."

Dodo was suddenly very interested. "Do tell."

"Well, I happened to hear them talking when they thought no one was listening. Veronica was spitting that he had better keep his end of the deal."

The gossip in Dodo awoke. "What did she mean?"

"No idea," replied Bunty. "But it looks like there may be trouble in paradise. If you ask me, I think he merely tolerates her, but I don't know why."

Curious. Dodo's brain started firing. What if Rupert knew Walter was coming and came along with Veronica to eliminate him?

It was time to get back to the serious matter at hand.

"Now, tell me about Granville."

Bunty was not a girl prone to blushing, but splotches of red appeared on her fleshy cheeks. "We met about three months ago at a county cricket match. He was one of the players for the opposing team." She pressed her hands together and stopped.

"And…" prodded Dodo.

"And what?"

"Oh, come on! I've never seen you interested in a man before. This is *big* Bunty!"

"Oh, all right." Her dull, commonplace face caught light as she prepared to tell her story. "He didn't play very well, if you must know, and in the tea tent afterward I decided to go and commiserate—you know appeal to his ego, tell him that there were some bad calls and all that sort of thing. He was grateful for my sympathies and we ended up chatting for ages. After a bit Bartie wanted to go and Granville offered to drive me home so that we could keep talking. It's not often I meet a man tall enough for me."

"Quite so," agreed Dodo, thinking that was certainly not his only qualification.

"We've been writing and telephoning—when the blasted thing is working—and have met up in town a couple of times."

"So, it's pretty serious?" asked Dodo.

"I hardly dare hope so," gasped Bunty, clasping her hands under her generous chin.

Dodo caught sight of the fog through the window and remembered that this was not just a schoolgirl chat. She cleared her throat.

"Given the present circumstances, I need to know a bit more background. Is that all right?"

Bunty nodded. "He's from Coventry and the only son of a duke. He has a couple of sisters who look just like him."

Poor girls.

"His father is very ill and expected to die at any moment, I believe. It's all rather sad. Granville didn't know if he'd be able to get away this weekend, but he's been so attentive to his father that his mother urged him to take some time for himself. They said they would call if the old boy took a turn for the worse."

Not on that *telephone.*

"So, he will soon be a duke," Dodo pointed out.

"I suppose so," said Bunty, chewing her lip. "I hadn't really thought about it."

Dodo was sure she had not. "And does this duchy come with money?"

Bunty leaned back throwing her hands up. "Pots of it! The Posts have always been very conservative with their money according to Granville. A bit stingy if you ask me." This was rich coming from Bunty whose family never spent a penny on anything unless they were forced to.

Bunty's father had died while the twins were still quite young, and her mother had followed suit while Bunty was in her teens, leaving her and Bartie with enough money that they did not have to think about it. The decaying house and skeleton staff were merely a matter of priorities.

A gale had kicked up outside, rattling the loose windows.

"And did Granville know any of these people before?"

"He had taken me to the opera where we first met Isabella. Granville is dotty about opera. I tolerate it myself, but he told me that Isabella was exceptional— and she was—and we waited to talk to her after the performance. They hit it off immediately. She is just finding her footing in England, and I think she realized that someone like Granville could help her career." Bunty took a sip of tea and winced, replacing it on the table.

"But does he know anyone else here, other than Bartie of course?"

"No, just me, Bartie, and Isabella."

A black bird swooped close to the window, coasting on the windy current, its feathers ruffled. If the wind picked up it might blow the fog away.

"Does Bartie like him?" asked Dodo.

Spotting a smudge on her shoe, Bunty licked her finger and rubbed it away.

"Very much. I think Daddy would approve too." Bunty had been much closer to her father than her mother. Lady Gillingsworth had never understood her Amazonian daughter.

"I'm sure he would," Dodo agreed. She ran her fingers through the pearls. "And what about Walter. How did he come to be here this weekend?"

"Well now, that is a little less straightforward," Bunty began. "He sort of invited himself too."

Dodo found that more than a little suspicious. "How so?"

"We met him in Cornwall some weeks ago. He was rather loud and obnoxious, and I gave him a wide berth, but he played cards with Bartie and lost badly."

"Yes, he mentioned that to me. He thinks Bartie let him win it back the next evening."

"Astute and true. You know Bartie, hates to hurt anyone's feelings. He's a tender boy. He told me he felt awful about it and decided to let Walter win it back." She picked at some skin that was hanging from the side of her scruffy nails.

"Anyway, that's really all the contact we had with him until he turned up at the pub in the village one night. He said he was in the area visiting a distant cousin and was on his way home. He brought his drink over to our table and started chatting as though we were old friends and somehow, we got around to the fact that we were having this long weekend and he inveigled an invitation. I remember that Bartie and I stared at each other in confusion. Neither one of us had invited him. Personally, I would rather he was not here but—oh!" She stopped mid-sentence, her bottom lip wobbling. "He's *not* here anymore. He's at the bottom of some dirty, muddy bog. Oh, what a frightful person I am! Forgive me."

Dodo patted Bunty's arm. "You are not a horrible person. Unpleasant people do not become paragons of virtue just because they have died. And you were nothing but pleasant to him. What is more, you stayed up all night and then went searching for him this morning. No one could have done more."

Bunty leaned forward and hugged her. "You always know how to make me feel better, Dodo. Even when we were little. I still have your Mr. Wiggles. Look!" She pointed to the bed where a very sorry looking bunny sat among the pillows.

"Good grief!" cried Dodo. "He's looking rather ragged. He must be, what? Fifteen years old?"

"He kept me company all through boarding school," admitted Bunty.

The clock in the hall chimed. Time to move things along.

"Right, just one last person. Isabella. Do you know anything about her background?"

"Hers is a rags-to-riches story," began Bunty. "She's the daughter of a corn farmer outside Barcelona. She grew up with few worldly goods, but her voice was so incredible that her parents sacrificed in order to pay for voice lessons with a master. It didn't take long for people to recognize her talents and she was soon singing all over Spain. Her singing master suggested that she try to gain international attention and arranged for her to sing in smaller locales with a view to eventually singing on a London stage."

Dodo marveled that Isabella had adapted so well that she was able to mix with the upper classes so seamlessly. "What a lovely tale. I suppose Granville's sponsorship could make all the difference."

They were interrupted by a knock on the door.

"It's me," said Bartie, slipping in. "Granville is asking for Bunty."

Bunty looked at Dodo.

"I think I'm done for now," she said. "You can go, and I can ask Bartie questions in here."

Bunty unfolded herself from the cozy chair. "Right-o."

"My turn in the hot seat," said Bartie with a grim smile.

Chapter 10

Bartie sat down in the chair Bunty had just vacated, pushing his round glasses up his button nose.

"Bunty has already told me details about your guests. What I want to know from you is any thoughts you might have about them. Let's start with the missing man."

Bartie twisted his mouth and scrunched his nose. "There is definitely something odd about him."

Dodo reflected on her own opinion of Walter. A dreadful letch. "Odd? What do you mean?"

Bartie hesitated. "Well, I hate to speak ill of the dead—or in this case, the missing."

Dodo smacked her pencil against the notebook. "Mystery solving is no time for holding things back, Bartie. Being polite will not help me at all."

Bartie sighed.

"Well, that obnoxious voice for a start. Sounded like a talking donkey." He chuckled. "No one really talks like that, do they? It was like he was trying too hard to fit in."

Bartie had hit the nail on the head.

"Yes, it was awful." Dodo agreed.

"And his manners were not quite up to snuff. Always making faux pas."

Dodo remembered the insolent way he had looked all the women up and down.

"How did you meet him?" she asked. Although she had already heard the story from his sister, she was interested in his take on things.

"I was playing cards at a friend's house in Cornwall. He watched me for a while before joining the game. Made me pretty self-conscious actually. I suppose he was trying to see if I had a tell or something. He lost horribly the first night, but I couldn't be absolutely sure he hadn't done it on purpose."

"Why on earth would anyone lose at cards on purpose?" asked Dodo with a frown.

"Exactly!" Bartie told her the story about letting Walter win back his money.

"You're such a dear," Dodo remarked. "Always have been."

Bartie smiled like a schoolboy and poured himself a cold cup of tea. Dodo waited for him to flinch as his lips hit the chilly liquid, but the smile never left his face. She had been brought up on piping hot tea. Anything less was considered an abomination.

"Walter was a decent card player, but I had the impression he wasn't really concentrating during that first game. He made some critical errors, and I took him for three hundred pounds. Shocking amount of money."

"Did he seem bothered by the loss?"

"I had the impression he was expecting it," said Bartie. "I can't put my finger on why. And he obviously doesn't have oodles of cash—his clothes are good quality but worn."

"How did he react the following evening when he won the money back?"

"He was playing much better the next time and his bets were smaller. He seemed relieved I would say. If he knew I let him win, he didn't let on."

Dodo thought about what Walter had told her about those card games in Cornwall, when they first met. He *had* suspected Bartie of helping him. And it hadn't hurt his pride. Most men would have been put out if they thought someone was suggesting they were incompetent by playing below their usual standards, but Walter had laughed about it.

"What happened after the second game finished?" Perhaps his actions revealed some embarrassment.

Bartie rubbed his nose. "He took his winnings and left quickly, actually."

"How did your friend know him?" asked Dodo.

"That's another peculiar thing," said Bartie, lifting his shoulder in a half shrug. "He didn't. We had gone to the local pub in the afternoon and Walter was alone, having a drink and started talking to us. My friend mentioned that we were playing cards later and must have invited him to join us."

A thought flashed in Dodo's brain. "Do you think perhaps Walter invited himself?"

Bartie studied the worn rug. "I'm not sure. I wasn't really in the circle of conversation at the time. Could have. Why do you ask?"

She tapped the lead of the pencil onto the paper. "Because Bunty said he invited himself to *this* weekend. Twice would lead me to deduce that these were not chance meetings."

Bartie held up his palms. "I say! Why ever would he do that?"

"That, my dear cousin, is the knotty question," she remarked, pointing her finger at him. "Did you see him interact with anyone outside of the drawing or dining rooms?"

Bartie shifted forward in the chair. "He did make an awkward play for Isabella in the hall. Totally bad form. She shut that down pretty quick. She is *far* too good for him." A whimsical smile drifted across his boyish face.

"She is very pretty," said Dodo, watching her cousin's eyes.

"She's beautiful. I don't think she would be interested in someone like me, though." Bartie blew out his cheeks. "I'm not manly enough. Not compared to someone like Rupert."

Dodo searched for a diplomatic answer. "Don't sell yourself short, Bartie. Show her your chivalrous side; open doors, slide out chairs, listen. Women love that."

His brow scrunched with doubt. "I tried but she resisted."

Dodo waved her hands around. "No, you rushed in like a clumsy bear and encroached on her space without an invitation. This calls for subtlety and patience."

Bartie had been prone to adolescent crushes where he smothered the girls he liked. It seemed that he had learned little from his youthful failures.

Bartie inclined his head. "So, you think I have a chance?"

He wasn't bad looking and he was fun to be with— a girl could do worse.

"I don't see why not," she said.

Bartie stroked his cherubic chin.

"Did Walter talk to anyone else that first night?" she continued.

"Not that I saw but I think he went straight to his room. I didn't see him again until he was persuading Bunty to go on a ramble after lunch the next day."

"So, you didn't see him say anything to Veronica?" She was hoping someone would corroborate Isabella's statement.

"No. Did he?" He was blinking rapidly.

"Apparently he was rather crude."

"Well, that's what I mean; no manners at all." He slouched back into the easy chair.

Dodo referred to her list. "Do you like Granville?"

He suddenly looked like a dog with two tails. "Oh yes! I like him because he makes Bunty happy. He's very sweet to her. If he were to propose I would not stand in the way."

"Well, that's a ringing endorsement, if you ask me," said Dodo. She checked her notes. "And what do you think of Veronica and her man?"

"Much too flashy for my taste," he said pulling his ear. "Nothing real about her. And she leads that poor chap a dog's life by all accounts."

"Poor chap?" cried Dodo, slapping the arm of the chair. "Poor judgement more like. He made his choice and now he has to live with it. Anyone can tell she's horrid."

"Woah!" cried Bartie. "That's a bit strong, Dodo. What did the poor chap ever do to you?"

Dodo puffed air. "Nothing. He merely showed up with my arch nemesis."

"Haha! I'm so used to you all sophisticated and full of confidence," said Bartie, chuckling. "It's rather funny to see how she affects you."

"I thought I'd never have to see her again," she responded, flicking the pages of the notebook.

"Do you remember how awkward you were at thirteen? Long gangly legs, teeth too big for your mouth and huge unruly eyebrows?"

She bit back a smile. "Don't remind me. I had a particularly bad awkward stage. And Veronica let me know it on a daily basis."

Bartie snorted. "Well, you are now the sun to her moon. You have your revenge I'd say."

"Oh, Bartie!" exclaimed Dodo, "That might be the nicest thing you've ever said to me."

Bartie blushed.

She was finding it hard to stay on track while questioning her relatives.

"Back to Rupert. Did you happen to see him talking in private to Walter?"

"No, sorry."

Could Isabella be lying about the heated exchange? She would need to interview Rupert and confront him about it.

"Not a problem." She closed the notebook. "I think that's it for now. If you remember anything, make sure to let me know."

"Will do." Bartie stood and jammed his hands into his front pockets. "Walter was a cad, but I do feel awful that he's missing. Like I said, the moors are terrifying at night. I keep hoping he'll stroll through the door at any moment." He crossed the room and touched Mr. Wiggles. "Do you want to talk to anyone else?"

"Yes. First, I want to ask Isabella about that moment with Walter. She didn't mention it. But I'll come downstairs in a bit and see if she's about."

When Bartie left, Dodo went to her room to freshen up. The effects of too little sleep were beginning to take their toll. She rang her bell and Lizzie appeared a few minutes later.

"Lizzie, do I look awful?" Dodo pulled the purple skin under her eyes.

Lizzie pursed her lips. "That right there, is a loaded question, m'lady."

Dodo frowned at herself in the mirror. "I'll take that as a 'yes'." She picked up some lipstick and brushed it over her mouth. "Would you be a dear and do something with my hair?"

Lizzie came over to the dressing table, reached for the brush and gently pulled it through Dodo's thick mane. She felt her shoulders relax and a stupor of exhaustion grip her.

"You spoil me, Lizzie," she murmured, closing her eyes.

"I am happy to do it, m'lady."

"Pick up any gossip below stairs?"

"About the missing guest? As a matter of fact, I did. The younger maid went up to set his fire and air his room the first night. She said he was a bit too friendly, if you get my drift, and she high tailed it out of there. But not before noticing he had a lot of luggage for a weekend."

Dodo struggled to open an eye. "That's interesting. He didn't seem much of a clotheshorse to me. I wonder why he brought so much?"

"She went to unpack it for him," Lizzie continued, "but he got angry and snapped that he would see to it. Then he seemed to realize that he had not been nice and that's when he got a bit frisky."

"You are a treasure trove of information, as always." Dodo's head sunk forward, too heavy to hold up.

"Shouldn't you take a nap, m'lady?"

Dodo hauled her head upright. "No. I'll be fine. Just need a second wind."

Lizzie stuck a pretty pearl pin into Dodo's hair. "Drowned. Such a terrible way to go!"

"Agreed. Horrible."

Lizzie tucked Dodo's hair under and sprayed one of the newly produced hair lacquers to hold it in place. "This damp air is not good for your style. Hopefully, this sticky stuff will help." She ran her fingers over Dodo's whole head. "But do *you* think Mr. Montague might have been pushed?"

"The rumor mill is hard at work then?" Dodo smirked. "I haven't said that in so many words, but there is the possibility. One of the guests said she saw Walter arguing with Veronica's fancy man."

"Fancy man? You mean Mr. Danforth? Oh, surely not! He's lovely, he is."

Dodo twisted around in her chair to lock eyes with her maid who looked like a love-struck teenager.

"Don't tell me you haven't noticed, m'lady," said Lizzie. "He is so handsome. He could be in the films, he could."

Amused at the effect Mr. Danforth was having on her maid, she cleared her throat. "One must question the intelligence of any

64

man who chooses to be in a relationship with Veronica. No matter how good he looks."

"So, you *did* notice!" Lizzie was beaming from ear to ear. "Don't you agree that he's rather magnificent?"

"That is beside the point, Lizzie. He allegedly argued with a man who is now presumed dead." And she had made the mistake of falling for a criminal before.

"Oh, Mr. Danforth couldn't have done anything," Lizzie remonstrated. "He's far too nice. He opened the door for me this morning." Dodo watched incredulously as Lizzie wrapped a small ringlet around her finger. "No gentleman has ever done that for me. Not even Mr. Bartie."

Dodo scowled. "He could just be trying to keep up appearances. He must know someone will put the pieces together soon. At this point, Mr. Danforth is the prime suspect."

"*If* Mr. Montague was pushed," Lizzie reminded her. "Are the police coming?"

"I called them early this morning but the fog is thick again and the phone is down."

"So, it's all up to you," Lizzie remarked.

"Well, I have you to help me, but yes. Essentially, it is up to me." She examined her hair.

"I'll ask some questions downstairs, see if anyone else heard the argument."

"That would be most helpful. I really need to know what the quarrel was about. If I ask Mr. Danforth, it's in his best interests to lie."

Dodo stood up and took a look in the long mirror. "Bunty thinks there's trouble in paradise anyway. She heard Veronica and Mr. Danforth arguing."

Lizzie's hands flew to her cheeks. "Really? I can ask the maids if they know anything."

Satisfied with her appearance, Dodo twirled. "Alright. Now, I'd better go down and continue the investigation. At some point I will have to interview Veronica. I'd rather have a cavity filled to be honest."

As she descended her stomach rumbled loudly and she realized she hadn't really eaten anything since her return that morning. Glancing at her watch she was shocked to see that it was already tea-time.

I hope Bunty has had the wherewithal to order it.

The smell of brewed tea and cakes drifted out as she opened the drawing room door and her mouth watered. All the remaining guests were gathered around the little tea table, balancing plates full of goodies, and teacups on knobbly knees. They looked up in unison rather as a dog that has been caught eating a cooling pie from the kitchen table.

"You don't think it's disrespectful, do you?" pleaded Bunty, sitting very close to Granville. Any closer and she would be in his lap.

"One has to eat," declared Dodo, "and I for one am famished." With her permission to indulge, the whole room relaxed.

The aging cook had outdone herself and Dodo remembered that she had teased Walter about her abilities on the night he arrived. She had the good graces to feel bad about it. Not bad enough to refrain from placing a delicate flaky pastry onto her plate, however.

Everyone was squished onto the furniture in front of the fire, which was roaring, so Dodo stepped behind one of the sagging chairs. She would worry about tea when she was done with the pastry.

Veronica's vicious chin jutted out as she sat at an angle from Rupert. Again, her clothes were impossibly ill conceived for a winter weekend in the depths of the Devon countryside—all silks and chiffon. *Did she think it was Wimbledon in June?*

Isabella had finally surrendered to the climate and borrowed some clothes from Bunty that Dodo remembered her aunt wearing long ago. They were vastly out of style and much too big, but they were warm and wooly. Isabella was quietly sipping tea with wide, ebony eyes framed with thick lashes. Bartie was making doe eyes at her, but she did not appear to notice. Granville and Bunty were talking, heads together, deep in some private conversation.

Mouth dry from the melt-in-your-mouth sweet cake, Dodo stepped round the chair and reached over to pour herself some tea.

Unfortunately, Rupert's foot was sticking out and before noticing, she tripped over it, clutching Bartie's shoulder to stop herself from falling.

"I am so terribly sorry," said Rupert, jumping up to help, his tone much less stiff than usual.

"She's fine, aren't you Dodo? Sit down Rupert," commanded Veronica, eyes hard as steel.

Rupert opened his mouth to speak, then thought better of it again, but not before Dodo noticed his ears were tinged with red.

"Yes, I'm fine," Dodo responded.

Pouring the tea, she returned to her place behind the chair. Veronica was talking nineteen to the dozen about nothing in particular but Rupert was staring at the fire, clearly not listening. Perhaps Bunty was right; the bloom could be off the rose.

Dodo searched each face in the room, hoping that Walter had not been pushed. They were all stuck together because of the fog and she didn't like the idea that one of these people could be a murderer.

In her experience, murderers were unpredictable.

She rolled her shoulders. It was time to talk to Rupert. She had unconsciously put it off, but she could not re-interview Isabella until it was done. She would leave interviewing Veronica until the last possible moment.

Catching Rupert's eye, she asked, "Might I have a private word?"

Chapter 11

Rupert's coloring was naturally pale like fresh cream, but her request sent it sliding down the color wheel. As he bit his lip, she noticed his right front tooth was slightly chipped. The tiny imperfection in an otherwise perfect face, rendered him more likeable, somehow.

He followed her out of the room into the hallway that felt like the polar ice cap in comparison to the warm, friendly drawing room. Dodo wrapped her arms around her body.

Pushing open the door to the library she immediately sensed that no fire had been lit and shrank back. The room was cold and still as a cellar. She would have to freeze.

Feeling the need to establish her authority, she chose to sit behind the desk and invited Rupert to take the chair on the other side. Who knew what lies Veronica had told him about her?

Gone was the confident, man-about-town who hung from Veronica's arm. Though he was still impeccably dressed in gray, wide, soft wool pants and a cashmere sweater, here sat a much less self-assured version. His charming face was clouded over with a concerned frown. He placed both elbows on the arms of the chair and clasped his hands tightly. He was obviously aware that the finger of suspicion was pointed directly at him.

How to begin? She would take her lead from Scotland Yard's Chief Inspector Blood. Direct and blunt.

"How did you know the missing man, Walter?"

Rupert's head thrust back slightly, and his lips parted in surprise. "I didn't know him." The light blue irises flared with genuine surprise.

She narrowed her eyes. "You were seen having an argument with him."

Rupert's shoulders relaxed and a devastating smile broke out over his classic features. She felt a little warmer.

"Oh that!" He laced his long fingers together. "Walter said something extremely inappropriate to Veronica and I told him to watch his mouth. No class at all. Actually, he's lucky I didn't give him a fat lip!"

Dodo pursed her lips. Walter was shaping up to be an utter rake. She thought of the way he had looked at her, the maid's testimony, the pass he made at Isabella and now this ugly interaction with Veronica. Was no woman safe?

Rupert's smile melted into a boyish, guileless grin, opening a window into a different person altogether. A person she might like to meet. She swallowed, forgetting why they were in the room.

No! He must be playing her. No one with an ounce of sense would spend five minutes with Veronica.

Dodo cleared her throat and looked anywhere but at him.

"So, you're saying that neither you nor Veronica had met him before?"

"No!"

She risked another look and found him resting his chin on his hand and studying her. It was not the kind of stare that made one uncomfortable. It was the sort that made you tingle all over. Which was completely inappropriate since he was here at Blackwood with another woman.

Focus.

"He was a perfect stranger," Rupert continued. "Frankly, I arrived knowing no one. I just came along for the ride because Vero—" The words that had tumbled out stopped abruptly. Dodo raised her brows and twisted her watch band. Waiting.

The twinkle that had lit up his eyes a moment before had vanished.

This man was confusing.

"I mean, Veronica was invited by Bunty and told that she could bring someone."

What secret did he swallow?

"How long have you known Veronica?" This wasn't strictly a question that was vital to the investigation—she was simply curious.

A brief pause and a flick of the eyes to the left told Dodo that he had taken a moment to answer. Truth needed no such pause.

"Quite a while now. We met after a polo match." He ran a nervous hand through his thick, sandy hair, unwilling to look Dodo in the eye. The tables had turned in just a few moments. Any trust he had earned was draining away.

"Can you tell me what happened during the walk on the moors? I understand you started out with a larger group but when I saw you come back to the house, you and Veronica were alone."

Again, a pause while his eyes darted around the book-filled room. Really, she was losing her patience.

He finally fixed his gaze on her, a line of concern between his eyes. "Rambling around the moors in November is not really Vero's thing, you know. She will kill me for telling you this, but we didn't really go."

The man wasn't making any sense. "Didn't go? But I saw you myself."

A look of resignation flashed across his perfect face.

"We went a little way with everyone but then Vero pulled me aside when the fog started to drop. She told me that there was no way she was going to get cold and wet and she had a plan. We hung back and hid behind an obliging grassy hillock. When you and Bartie passed by on your way out, we slipped back to the gardens and waited in the shed. As the fog thickened up, she told me that I was fortunate that we had not gone on as it could be dangerous. Personally, I would have enjoyed the adventure but..."

Dodo softened her face. He was lying to protect Veronica. "I know. Opposing Veronica takes a lot of energy."

He tipped his head and her breath caught. "I forgot," he said. "You knew her at school."

Dodo sucked in a deep breath. "Yes. We were not bosom buddies."

"Well, then you know it is easier to comply. She had smuggled out some brandy in her coat and that warmed us up as we waited. We heard you and Bartie as you came back into the garden and I was ready to follow you, but Veronica suggested we be the last to return so as not to raise suspicion. We waited until we saw Bunty, Granville and Isabella and then I said I'd had enough. That's when we made our dramatic entrance as though we had been left out on the moors."

The cheat!

"If you are telling the truth..."

The return of Rupert's radiant smile came close to convincing her of his innocence.

"If?"

"I have to remain objective, Mr. Danforth."

"Please. Call me Rupert."

She rearranged her pearls. "Mr. Danforth. Rupert. If you are telling the truth, this points back to Walter's disappearance being the result of an accident since you were nowhere near him at the time he went missing. I suppose Veronica will corroborate your statement?"

Rupert clasped his hands together and rested them on his bottom lip, eyes serious. "Oh dear. Then I may have a problem. Vero is all about saving face so I very much doubt she will admit to this. Especially to you. She will probably spin some tale about wandering around fearing for her life, but I assure you, I *am* telling the truth. Walter may have been a cad, but I would never hurt another person."

As Rupert pleaded, his crystal blue eyes overflowed with innocence, drawing her in.

He suddenly slapped the arm of the chair breaking their connection. "I think I can prove it!" he said with fervor. "I believe we left our glasses in the shed. You could check my alibi that way." He snapped his fingers. "And you and Bartie passed very near the shed on your way back and I saw that you were limping though I could not see why. How would I know that if I was still out on the moors?"

He had a point. Between this statement and the fact that Bunty had been with Walter *after* she lost sight of Veronica and Rupert, Dodo was convinced.

"Can you think of anything else that might be useful?" She hoped not. She did not want to spend any more time alone with this man she had decided to dislike. Attraction was growing in her like a weed in fertilizer. This interview needed to end and soon.

"Yes! As we were leaving the shed, I thought I heard the sound of someone else moving across the grass. I peered around to see who it was, but the fog was coming in swirls and I could see nothing at that point. It was probably just one of the dogs."

He sat back in the chair, his lean, muscular frame filling his sweater in all the right places.

He is off-limits. For so many reasons.

"Well, thanks for your candor," she said. "I am convinced that you are telling the truth because it corroborates someone else's statement and will inform the group that we can assume that Walter's fall was the result of an unfortunate accident." And this way she would be able to avoid an interview with Veronica.

"You mean, I'm no longer the prime suspect?" A dangerously flirtatious smile bloomed across his features sending heat through her bloodstream.

This would not do. He was telegraphing very mixed signals which was sending her emotions all over the place. As much as she disliked Veronica, he *was* her boyfriend and as such it was inappropriate of him to tease her. She did not approve of unfaithfulness; it showed a weakness of character that she could not countenance.

She looked away to discourage him, running her eyes around the old maps on the wall but when she risked a look back at him the smile was waiting for her, displaying the endearing chipped tooth that rendered his striking features more approachable. She felt a sudden impulse to ask how he had chipped it, an impulse she quickly buried.

Her manner must have transmitted her disapproval of his flirting because his tapered cheekbones flattened as though a mask had slipped back into place.

What on earth is going on?

Confused by so many alternating emotions, she jumped up, concluding the interview, and Rupert released his tall frame from the chair. He walked over and opened the library door, his palm on the handle, waiting for Dodo to exit. As she walked through, mere inches from him, a complicated mixture of electric charge and disdain washed over her, cluttering her chest and mind with a riot of bewildering feelings.

Flustered, she paused.

The desire to look back at him was surprisingly strong but she reminded herself that he had chosen Veronica and swiped the temptation away. Hurrying back to the drawing room she felt relief to be back among the gaggle of bodies that still sat around the teapot.

Rushing over to the chair she had claimed before the interview, she grabbed the back of it like a crutch. Out of the corner of her eye she saw Rupert return to sit by Veronica whose suspicious gaze darted between them.

Dodo directed her comments to the fireplace. "I no longer believe that Walter's death was anything other than an accident and that is what I will tell the police when they are able to get here."

"I could have told you that!" spat Veronica. "Really, I expected more from the famous detective I've heard about."

Still catty.

The knowledge that Veronica had wiggled out of the walk on the moors rushed to the tip of Dodo's tongue. But disclosing that now would be petty. Veronica was baiting her just like she did at school, and to retaliate would be to descend to Veronica's level. Instead, she realized that this secret gave her power that she could wield at an opportune moment.

Dodo had matured.

Veronica apparently had not.

The vulgar tension was thick, and Bunty stumbled to disperse it. "Well, that's a relief, Dodo," she gushed, "but since poor Walter is dead, I think a simple dinner and early night might be in order out of respect."

Granville cleared his throat and everyone in the room looked his way. "May I suggest asking Isabella to sing something appropriate for the occasion?" he suggested.

"I think that's a lovely idea," agreed Bunty. "What do you say, Isabella?"

The Spanish singer's black eyes looked out from her delicate heart-shaped face as she pushed back her wonderful, web of raven curls.

"I would be honored to," she whispered, smiling at Granville. "I can sing something to honor the dead man."

"That's settled then," said Bunty. "Dinner at seven-thirty followed by a performance."

73

§

Dodo really wanted to take a bath to consider the events of the long day but sharing a bathroom with the others in this wing, made such a request impossible as everyone needed to dress for dinner. She cursed her cousins' thrift. Instead, Lizzie filled her china bowl with warm water and Dodo used a soft, wet cloth to wipe away the strains of the day before taking a well-deserved nap.

When Lizzie returned an hour later, Dodo jolted awake from a deep sleep, her heart leaping to her throat.

"Sorry, m'lady," said Lizzie. "I can come back later if you like."

Dodo's mouth was dry, and her tongue felt cottony as she rubbed her eyes. "No, I need to get up or I won't sleep tonight. It will just take me a minute to fully wake."

"Well, here's a nice cup of tea to help." Lizzie placed a tray on the bed and went to open the curtain. The day was fading, and the wall of fog did not allow the faint light to penetrate. She switched on the light.

"Lizzie, you are an angel, I'm parched." Dodo reached for the cup. "I didn't get a lot of sleep last night and my body must have thought I was down for the night."

Lizzie began arranging things on the dressing table.

"Come and sit on the bed, Lizzie and let's chat." Dodo plumped her pillow and sat with her back against the headboard while her maid sat on the end of the bed.

"I found out that Mr. Danforth did not know Walter before this weekend and that the argument was in defense of Veronica's honor." Dodo snorted.

Lizzie raised her brows. "You've changed your tune. I thought you had assumed he was going to lie through his teeth."

Dodo had the grace to feel penitent. "I still think he must be a very silly man, but I have to admit, I did believe him when he explained everything."

"Could it have anything to do with those baby blues?" Lizzie wiggled her eyebrows.

"Of course not!" Dodo was aware that she was being overly defensive. "I am much more professional than that. Besides, he

74

admitted that he and Veronica doubled back in the fog and waited things out in the garden shed with some brandy. I was going to ask you to look for evidence that they were there. Trust but verify."

Lizzie started to get up. "That sounds more like you. Shall I pop down before it gets too dark?"

"Heavens no! No one will go there tonight so I think it's safe to wait until the morning."

"Good." Lizzie dropped back to the bed. "It's very creepy out there."

"My conclusions are that Walter must have slipped and drowned. He wasn't a terribly nice man, by all accounts, but it is still a horrid way to die and we should find out if he has any next of kin and let them know as soon as we can."

Dodo swung her legs round, pushing the tea tray away and stepped off the bed, stretching like a sleepy baby. "Did you hear that Isabella is going to entertain us tonight. I don't think I asked you to bring anything suitable for the opera, did I?"

Lizzie beat the air with her hands. "No, but I packed something special anyway. You never know, I say."

Dodo hugged her maid. "You are the best!" She sat down at the dressing table and examined her tired face with a frown. "Which one did you bring?"

"The white and gold Valérie Sourdais from the House of Dubois."

Dodo twisted in her seat and clapped her hands. "My absolute favorite!"

Tonight, Dodo was determined to outshine Veronica and the white and gold dress was the perfect way to do it. Looking fabulous was the best revenge. She spread cold cream over her face to moisten it and then applied make-up as if she were going to a fashion show in Paris. Black kohl to rim her eyes, accentuating the deep blue irises, red lipstick to draw attention to her natural cupid's bow and a light dusting of powdered rouge for her cheeks. She even employed an eyebrow pencil and some of the new, caked mascara. Satisfied with the look, she allowed Lizzie to step in and set her hair.

Once the gown had been slipped on, Dodo took a minute to admire her reflection. The off-white, fit-and-flare dress barely brushed the floor with the finest of netting that hung from the knee. The v-neck was embellished with gold and silver sequins that trailed in vines down the bodice and around the hips. It was new from the house of Dubois but had been designed by a young model who had been killed for her genius. Proceeds from the sale of the dress were being used to educate underprivileged designers in her honor.

"I shall need a stole or wrap," she said as Lizzie handed her a white mink that wrapped around the shoulders and snapped with a diamond clip in the front.

"Perfect!"

"Watch out Mr. Danforth!" murmured Lizzie.

"I am *not* interested," Dodo protested as she stepped out the door. "Besides, I don't poach other girls' men—unlike some people."

"If you say so," retorted Lizzie with a cheeky grin.

Chapter 12

Dodo experienced a pleasant tingle of anticipation from her head to her toes, the instant before entering the room.

Everyone but Isabella was already down, scattered about the huge room with cocktails in hand.

It was immediately obvious that Veronica was trying too hard. She was gussied up in an absurd white chiffon gown trimmed with ostrich feathers and a matching turban. It was a dress more appropriate poolside in the Bahamas. To make matters worse, her make-up had been applied with a heavy hand. The effect was clownish. Dodo felt a secret delight at the spectacle.

Veronica certainly brings out the feline in me.

"Oh Dodo! You look positively adorable!" said Bunty, moving toward her in a large red taffeta gown with an oversize bow on the hip, and offering her a cocktail with an olive on the top.

Veronica took a sip from her glass that must have been full of pickle juice by the squinty look on her face. "Sequins, Dodo. How quaint."

Dodo explained the story behind the dress while everyone, except Veronica, was spellbound.

"Murdered over some sketches!" remarked Granville. "How tragic."

"Yes, it was and to boot she was an exquisitely beautiful girl," added Dodo.

"It is a great shame when the young die," agreed Bunty whose hair had been wrestled into a frizzy chignon. "Such a waste of talent."

Veronica placed her hand possessively on Rupert's knee who flinched at her touch. "Where is the diva?" she asked, tucking a stray hair under the awful turban.

As if summoned, Isabella entered, resplendent in a traditional scarlet flamenco dress, her hair pinned back with a red rose. Dodo heard Bartie gasp behind her.

"I say!" said Granville, holding Bunty's hand. "You look marvelous, my dear."

Isabella dipped her head and batted long, black eyelashes. "Why, thank you."

The gong sounded.

"Dinner is ready," declared Bunty unnecessarily. She and Granville led the way followed by Veronica and Rupert. Dodo winked at Bartie to encourage him to invite Isabella, and Dodo brought up the rear.

The dingy dining room had been brought back to life by silver candelabras on the table and the old chandelier bursting with candles. The table had been set with shining silver that was at least one hundred years old. It sparkled in the flickering light.

Mrs. Brown had outdone herself with a prawn mousse that melted on the tongue. Everyone agreed that it was the best they had ever tasted, and the wine flowed freely. Dodo was always careful to watch her intake as she abhorred losing control, but she could not help noticing that Veronica was not half so disciplined. Every time her glass was re-filled, Rupert cast a worried eye.

By the time the crêpes-suzette were served for dessert, Veronica was positively sloshed, and her turban sat askew.

"I'm not terribly sorry that Walter is gone," Veronica began as the flames leaped up from the pancakes.

The whole table stopped their conversations and stared at her.

"What?" she cried, pushing the turban too far the other way. "He said some awful things about me, didn't he Rupert?"

The picture portrayed by Rupert's sunken shoulders told a thousand words. "He did. But he didn't deserve to die, Vero."

"No one says such things to me without paying for it." Her hand was unsteady, and the wine was sloshing onto the clean, white cloth. "Horrible manners deserve to be punished," she continued, pushing her fork into the brandy-soaked hotcakes. "But you defended my honor, darling."

Dodo kept her eye on Rupert who was clenching his teeth while playing with a gold watch at his wrist. "Anyone would have done the same," he mumbled.

"But you are my little pookey." Veronica was on a roll and completely uninhibited. She walked her fingers unsteadily up the arm of Rupert's white dinner jacket to his shoulder and then touched the tip of his nose.

Rupert recoiled but Veronica didn't seem to notice.

Everyone went back to their own conversations, but Dodo was taking far too much pleasure in studying the couple on the other side of the table. Veronica waved at the servant to refill her glass.

"I say, old thing. Don't you think you've had enough?" Rupert's expression was as flat as the dessert on his plate.

"I'm just getting started," she responded with a gentle slap on his arm. Rupert's full lips narrowed into a thin, white line.

The servants removed the dessert china and brought in coffee. Rupert closed his eyes, tilting his fair head back.

"Sir?"

He snapped his eyes open. "Yes please. And she'll have some too."

Veronica began to giggle. "As long as it has something stronger added to it."

Rupert locked eyes with the servant and shook his head slightly, then his blue eyes bounced in Dodo's direction bursting with an unspoken apology.

In spite of her resolve to dislike him, Dodo smiled back, tipping her head toward Veronica.

Rupert's nose wrinkled and she laughed quietly into her coffee as they shared a joke at Veronica's expense.

Bartie struck his glass with a silver spoon and got to his feet.

"Time for the main event, ladies and gentlemen. If everyone would follow me back to the drawing room."

The hallway was as cold as Norway in February and Dodo hurried along, eager to get back to the warm. Her dress was devastatingly gorgeous, yes, but it was not suited for frosty, English manors.

The drawing room had been re-arranged while they were gone with chairs placed in a half-circle in front of the piano. The roaring fire delivered its heat and Dodo felt her tense muscles relax. She took the chair on one end, nearest the fireplace.

Rupert and Veronica sat at the other end, with everyone else, but Isabella, in between. Veronica was slumped in her chair, turbaned head on Rupert's shoulder, the large feather tickling his face.

Isabella stood in front of the piano.

Rupert pushed Veronica gently on to Bartie and jumped up, extending his hands.

"I thought it might be appropriate to have a minute of silence for Walter before we begin," he said. His sincerity could not be doubted and Dodo's first impression of him battled with this updated version of the man. She felt like Lizzie Bennet trying to figure out the character of Mr. Darcy when she said, '*I hear such different accounts of you as puzzle me exceedingly.*'

"He may not have been the most honorable of men but dying alone in a bog is a wretched way to go," finished Rupert.

"Here, here," mumbled the group.

Dodo watched as Rupert sat down and guided Veronica's drunken head back onto his shoulder.

In the silence, the cracking of the fire and the soft, regular breathing of Veronica were the only sounds. Dodo brought back the image of the felt hat and the red scarf floating in the liquid mud. She brought her hand to her throat.

After a minute, Bartie nodded at Isabella.

"I will sing for you, *La Mamma Morta* out of respect for the passing of our fellow guest, Walter Montague." She moved over to the piano keys and pressed one note then stood in front of the group, hands clasped together. Dodo braced. She was not a fan of opera.

The moment the first note escaped Isabella's mouth a sacred peace descended on the room. Her voice was like snowflakes falling on Christmas Eve. It inspired an emotional response and Dodo was transfixed. No one moved or shifted in their seat as the magic notes floated around the room.

When Isabella finished no one dared move for fear of breaking the spell. Even applause seemed sacrilegious. After several moments of silence, Isabella dropped her hands and smiled. "Did you like it?"

"Like it?" cried Bartie, jumping up to kiss her hand. "I imagine all the heavenly angels are mad with jealousy. You were marvelous!"

Isabella grabbed his face and placed two European kisses on his cheeks. Bartie lit up like a red chili pepper.

Dodo had been in a state of enchanted trance and took a moment to return to the here and now. She saw that the others were reflecting similar sentiments, except Veronica who was fast asleep draped over Rupert.

"Congratulations!" said Dodo, grasping Isabella by the shoulders. "I have never been a real lover of opera, but you have converted me. That was sublime!"

"You are too kind," blurted Isabella without the least hint of modesty. She was good and she knew it.

Granville was hot on Dodo's heels and pumped Isabella's hand. "Heavenly!" he declared. "When the London audiences hear you, your life will change forever."

"With you as a patron, I do believe so, Mr. Post."

Rupert slid out from under Veronica's cheek, laid her softly along two chairs and went to congratulate the petite Spaniard. Then they all gathered around the fire and Bunty turned off the main lights. The music had bewitched everyone, and they all sat in the quiet, watching the flames dance.

The entire experience was a fitting ode to the dead man.

§

Dodo stumbled down to breakfast at ten o' clock the next morning. It had been close to three in the morning when the party of dozing guests had gone to bed. Veronica had slept through the whole evening and as Dodo watched Rupert scoop her into his arms to take her up to her room, she felt an unexpected tug on her heart.

This morning, only Bunty and Bartie were in the breakfast room, their plates piled high with eggs and bacon.

"Hello!" said Bunty. "You're the first one up."

81

"Really?" she replied. She poured herself some tea and sat at the table with them. "What a memorable evening that was," she purred.

"I know," agreed Bunty, her hair sticking out in all directions, purple smudges under her eyes. "Granville asked if he could have a private meeting with me this morning. I think the music made him feel romantic." Bunty's green eyes sparkled.

"You think…?" asked Dodo.

"I do!" replied Bunty, her ruddy cheeks fit to burst. "And I will!"

Dodo enveloped her in a hug. "Congratulations, cousin. I'm very happy for you."

Isabella entered and Bunty withdrew into herself and her food, a secret smile dancing on her lips. Bartie knocked his chair over in his enthusiasm to greet her. "Good morning, Isabella. What can I get for you?"

Next, looking fresh in tweeds and a chunky argyle sweater, Rupert came in leading a drooping Veronica. Her eyes were smudged and her skin pale and clammy. She shielded her face from the dim morning light, faint stress lines fanning her cheeks.

She plonked herself in a chair. "Coffee!" she commanded Rupert.

He obliged, placing a cup of steaming black liquid in front of her. "Is it really still foggy?" she complained, running a hand through her flat, un-styled hair. "Does the bally sun ever shine in this awful place?"

Bunty looked as though she had been slapped. "It's supposed to brighten up tomorrow according to the radio."

"Tomorrow!" screeched Veronica. "I really wish I'd never come."

Me too.

Glancing at Rupert, Dodo saw a fleeting look of longsuffering. Perhaps the strain of this weekend would spell the end of their relationship.

"I was expecting a jolly fun time with lots of laughs," Veronica continued, "and all I've done is—"

A scream split the air.

Bartie ran out of the room and the guests all looked at each other in fear and confusion.

"Molly probably saw a mouse," Bunty explained, dipping toast in her tea.

Within minutes Bartie was back, skin white as the moon.

"Granville is dead."

Chapter 13

Bunty knocked her tea all over the tablecloth, the brown stain spreading like blood.

"What do you mean?" asked Dodo.

"What I said," declared Bartie. "Granville has died. The scream was from the maid. She went in to make up his bed but didn't get an answer when she knocked. She assumed he was already down for breakfast and went in. When she drew back the curtains, there he was, blue and cold."

"Ahhh," cried out Bunty clutching her heart. Bartie ran to her side and took her in his arms.

"No one move," commanded Dodo.

"Who does she think—" Dodo was up the stairs in a split second and didn't hear the end of Veronica's objections.

The room was still, cold, and lifeless—just like the corpse in the bed. Bartie's description had been spot on. Poor Granville was, in fact, blue. His lips were purple. There could be no doubt that he was dead.

Two 'accidental' deaths in three days were too much of a coincidence.

Dodo dropped to the ground and studied the floor. It was polished oak with a once thick Turkish rug on top. There were little bits of mud, some thread, a small piece of red yarn and a tiny white feather. She could hear Bunty's wailing rising up through the floorboards.

Moving to the bed she leaned over and examined the dead man's face. His expression was not peaceful, but his eyes were closed.

Thank heavens for small mercies.

Granville had either died of something like a painful heart attack, or he had been murdered.

She found a pencil on the desk and carefully pulled back the covers. One leg was bent but the other was straight. His fists were balled tight.

She carefully examined the outline of his head and stopped sharp. Granville had a long, white hair protruding from his nose.

Surely, he's too young to have a white nose hair.

Steeling herself, she bent her face close to his nose. She wished she had thought to grab her magnifying glass. The hair was fine, but something was wrong. She ducked down to the floor again and picked up the small feather she had seen, bringing it up to Granville's nose for comparison.

Not a hair.

She searched around for a pair of tweezers and found some in Granville's traveling case. Going back to the body she carefully extracted the foreign object.

It was part of a feather.

It lay in her hand like a witness against a death by natural causes.

The peace that had replaced her worry yesterday, slid back like a theater curtain revealing a drama.

One of the other guests was a cold-blooded murderer.

She pulled the bell next to the bed. Minutes later a maid came and hovered by the door.

"Please send Lizzie Perkins."

The maid beat a hasty retreat and Lizzie returned a few minutes later.

"Oh!" said Lizzie, her hand to her mouth. She had helped with several of Dodo's investigations, but she was still queasy around dead bodies. "Was he…you know…?"

"Murdered?" finished Dodo, poised over the body. "I believe so. I need you to bring me something to put evidence in. Don't tell anyone what you are doing. I don't want the murderer to know that I suspect foul play. They have taken care to make this seem like a natural death. If it wasn't for my experience, I would certainly accept that as the cause. But here we are, stranded at Blackwood with a murderer and we do *not* want to alert them. If they feel cornered, they may strike again. We're all safer if we pretend to accept that this death was natural, until the police get here—oh, and let's try calling them again. The stupid telephone wasn't working yesterday."

Lizzie had not set a foot into the room and fled down the stairs.

Curling her hand around the feather from the dead man's nose, Dodo started a thorough search of Granville's room. She found the usual clothing articles, washing and shaving items and a pair of boots next to some dress shoes. Inside a leather travel wash kit, she found a small blue box containing a simple diamond ring.

Her heart dropped.

"Here you go," said Lizzie, panting. Dodo slipped the ring into her pocket as Lizzie held out a small brown bag. Dodo placed the partial feather into it.

"Fold it over a couple of times. Do you have another?"

"I brought four, just in case," said Lizzie handing over the others.

"Good thinking!"

Into another one, Dodo put the full feather and into a third, the small piece of red yarn. She folded the tops and handed them to Lizzie.

"Hide these in my room and make sure you don't mention anything downstairs. Remember, we want everyone to believe we think his death was natural." She slipped the other bag in her pocket. "What about the police?"

"The phone is still down," explained Lizzie.

"Drat!" Dodo looked out the window. The fog was still unusually thick. "I suppose they couldn't get here anyway. Looks like it's just you and me."

One of Lizzie's eyebrows went up in panic. "I'm in a house with a killer and you want me to investigate the murder?"

"Shhh," warned Dodo quietly. "As long as the murderer doesn't feel threatened, I think we're safe."

Dodo moved over to the body and pulled the sheets up over the face. "You go and hide those clues, and I will go and face Bunty."

"What do you mean?" Lizzie's brows were knit in confusion.

Dodo pulled out the blue box and opened it. "She was right. Granville was going to propose today."

§

A low moaning sound, like a cow in labor, was coming from the settee. Bartie sat next to Bunty who was rocking back and forth, her tooth almost biting through her lip to stem the tide of tears. Dodo sat beside her, pulling her into a tight embrace.

After several minutes Bunty withdrew, pushing damp hair out of her eyes. "What happened? Can I see him?"

Addressing the whole group Dodo said, "I think Granville must have died of a heart attack or an aneurysm." Everyone started murmuring. She turned back to Bunty. "It wasn't a...peaceful passing. I don't recommend seeing him. Better to remember him as he was." She pulled the box out of her pocket and handed it to Bunty who lifted round eyes swimming in tears.

"Is this...?"

"Open it."

The diamond sat in the blue velvet, winking in the overhead light.

Bunty's eyes shot back to Dodo's. "I was right." She pried the ring out and slid it onto her finger. It fit perfectly and she clasped the ring to her heart.

"I am so sorry," Dodo whispered.

"What do we do now?" asked Rupert, coming to stand in front of Dodo, his hands in his pockets.

"We tried calling the police, but the line is still down," she explained. "And this fog is just sitting on us making it impossible to go to them."

"You expect me to stay in a house with a dead body?" cried Veronica, hysteria building as her nails picked at an invisible blemish.

"What do you suggest?" said Dodo calmly.

Veronica jutted out her bottom lip, eyes darting from side to side. "Can't we put him outside?"

Dodo moved out of Bunty's earshot and addressing Rupert, dropped her voice. "We should not move anything before the police arrive. With no fire in his room, it will stay pretty cold, so decay should not be an immediate problem."

"Two bodies in one weekend is rather a coincidence," said Isabella putting into words Dodo's own conclusions. "Are you sure he died of natural causes?"

Dodo looked at all the faces to judge how this statement was taken. Veronica grabbed Rupert's arm, her face erupting with fear.

"Quite sure," affirmed Dodo. "We technically have one missing person and one death. I'll probably ask some questions like I did after Walter's disappearance so that I can give a full report to the police."

"It gives me the heebie-jeebies anyway," moaned Veronica, still gripping Rupert's arm, her knuckles white. "Perhaps this house is cursed? It does look like the haunted houses in the movies."

"Now, now," said Dodo. "Panicking will not help the situation."

Rupert led Veronica to one of the old chairs and put his arm around her. Isabella sunk onto the other threadbare armchair looking small and vulnerable.

"Bunty, are you up to answering some more questions?" asked Dodo.

Like a robot, Bunty nodded and walked to the door following Dodo who led her up the stairs.

"I know we talked before, Bunty, but I think it's a good idea to go over things again. While your memory is fresh."

Bunty nodded chewing on an old handkerchief.

"You met Granville at a cricket match. You had never met him before, correct?"

Bunty shook her head.

"You said his father is ill and Granville is the next in line. And he is the only son, right?"

"Yes, Granville is the only son. No spare."

Dodo took a breath. A lot was riding on the next question. "Do you have any idea who the title will go to now?"

Bunty's bottom lip pulled down in a frown, tears building up in her eyes. "Not a clue. Perhaps there's a cousin in the bushes."

Not the answer she was hoping for.

"Tell me about last night," said Dodo. "What happened after we all split up?"

"Granville took me to my room and…" Her eyes welled again. "He gave me the most delicious kiss and then said, 'Until tomorrow. I need to ask you something'. And I watched him walk to his room. He went in and I heard a noise, like someone falling and he popped back out laughing that he had tripped over his boot that was right near the door."

An idea sparked in Dodo. "Is that like him? Is he untidy as a rule?"

Bunty blew into the handkerchief and wiped her cheeks. "No. He served in the war and I have never met a tidier person. Everything put in its place with precision. Nothing like me."

Dodo thought back to the room she had searched. Bunty was right, everything including the boots were neatly stored. So why had one boot been out of place the night before?

"And he didn't know anyone else here this weekend but you, Bartie, and Isabella."

"That's right."

Dodo tapped her chin with a finger. A theory was nudging its way into her brain. "Can you think of anything else that is out of place in the house?"

Bunty squeezed her eyes shut. "Mrs. Brown mentioned that some bread, cheese and milk were missing. She asked me to tell the guests that they are welcome to take what they need but to leave her a note so that she knows whether to buy more supplies. I forgot all about that."

Dodo's theory began to lose its teeth. "I suppose that's not very unusual. People get peckish in the night and search for some munchies."

Bunty suddenly raised anxious eyes. "Oh, and a couple of balls of knitting wool went walkabout. I noticed it when I got the orange one to help us in our search for Walter, remember?"

The little hairs on the back of Dodo's neck stood up. "What color was it?"

"Red."

A bell started to clang in Dodo's head.

Bunty twisted the ring on her finger. "I never thought I would get married, Dodo. I'm such an ungainly thing. Not like you and Didi, all dainty sophistication. Granville was a dream come true. He didn't care about all that. He loved my soul. That's what he told me." She put her head in her hands and wept. For the next

89

twenty minutes Dodo sat comforting a beloved cousin whose life had just been ruined forever.

Chapter 14

The time had come.

Dodo could not put it off any longer.

She *had* to interview Veronica.

Dodo would more willingly have had a tooth extracted without anesthesia than talk to Veronica one on one, but it had to be done now that a second suspicious death had occurred.

Why was Veronica really here?

Dodo decided to conduct the interview in the ramshackle library where she could put a bit of space between them and have the upper hand. She had asked a maid to make a fire to take the chill off. Dodo waited on one side of the scarred, Victorian desk for Veronica to enter. She sat down on the other side her hands clasped around her knees. Her eyes were still bloodshot from the previous night's over-indulgence and Dodo was gratified to see that she was tense.

Good.

She was still wearing the light dress but had found a man's chunky cardigan and slipped it over the top. The thought that it was Rupert's rankled.

Keep your mind on the task at hand.

Formality would provide a layer of armor.

"You met Bunty recently and she invited you to this weekend. Correct?"

Veronica unclasped her hands to chew on a brightly polished nail. "Yes. We met at a polo match and hit it off. I was there to support Rupert, and Bunty was sitting next to me."

"Do you often stay with people you have just met?"

That came out a little harsher than I intended.

Veronica pouted. "Yes. Don't you? I feel that one has to broaden one's narrow horizons."

"Actually, I prefer to know the people I am staying with," countered Dodo.

They were like two lionesses circling each other.

"I admit that I might have declined the invitation had I known how remote this place was—and how cold." Veronica's mouth curled. "Are they hard up for money?"

Dodo shuffled some books around on the desk.

"The plumbing is so primitive," Veronica continued. "I'm used to ensuite, myself."

"Bunty and Bartie are unspoiled by wealth," Dodo said in defense of her relatives. "They are content with things the way they are and see no need to update. It is a personal choice not a financial one."

She gripped the arms of her chair. "How long have you known Rupert?"

Veronica narrowed her eyes. "Why?"

"Let me ask it another way," she said. "Do you know him very well?"

Veronica's eyes flashed to the smoke-stained ceiling. "Yes. We've been together for *ages*. I think he's going to pop the question soon, as a matter of fact."

Really?

Dodo decided to test the veracity of this statement. "So, you know all about his family and history?"

Veronica shifted in her chair. "Well, I haven't met his family as such, but I've heard all about them. He has two sisters, both younger, and one is still at school. Julia and Margot."

Dodo remained unconvinced. "Where is he from?"

Veronica tilted her head, grasping at her neck. "Ummm, all over. Moves around a lot. Look, what has all this got to do with two dead men?"

Dodo rested her chin in her hand and directed a level gaze at Veronica who was constantly moving around in the chair.

"It's background research," Dodo lied. "The police will want to know all about us for when they write up their report."

"Then shouldn't you ask *Rupert* these things?"

"I did," said Dodo with a Cheshire cat smile. "But I need to verify people's statements. It might surprise you to know how dishonest people can be. Especially in situations like this."

"Oh." Guilt fanned across Veronica's face, and the nail went back to her mouth.

Dodo made a great show of writing something down. "And how many of the other people do you know?"

"No one. Well, you. And I forgot that I actually heard Isabella sing last year in a little hidey hole place, but I wouldn't say I know her."

Dodo tapped the desk with her fingers. "Tell me what Walter said to you."

"What?" Her cheeks took on the hue of the crimson drapes around them.

Dodo made a circle in the air with her finger. "When Rupert defended your honor."

Veronica waved a hand around. "Oh that! Walter made some crude remark about my bottom if you must know. Horrid man. It's just like when—" Veronica stopped abruptly, pursed her lips and plucked at her dress.

"You'd met him before?" asked Dodo wondering what she had almost said.

"No. No, it's just you know how men can be. I've suffered similar remarks in the past. With a figure like mine, it's bound to happen!" Her smile didn't quite reach her eyes.

Dodo decided to shake the tree.

"You came back early from the walk I understand."

Veronica froze. "Uh, we got back after Bunty and Granville. You were there in the mudroom."

"That is true, but I have since learned that you actually back-tracked and holed up in the garden shed and waited it out there."

"I…uh…" Veronica was blinking rapidly.

"Look, we found the empty bottle of brandy you took to keep warm and two small shot glasses, one with your shade of lipstick on it." Lizzie had retrieved them before breakfast.

Veronica's shoulders slumped. "Oh. I suppose it's no secret that I'm not really the country bumpkin type and with the drizzle and the fog it was more than I could bear. But I didn't want to be a party-pooper, so we sneaked back. No crime there." She forced a giggle.

Dodo doodled a circle on her notepad. "I know it was hard with the fog but did you see or hear anything unusual while you were in the shed?"

The concern slid from Veronica's face and she beamed as if she were being offered her choice of the crown jewels. "I was a little busy, if you get my drift."

It was all Dodo could do not to roll her eyes.

Leaning forward Veronica placed her hand on the desk. "Look Dodo, let's just put all that old school stuff behind us. What do you say?"

Dodo could hardly believe her ears. All the bullying at school had been one-sided and anger flared, burning Dodo from the inside out. This woman, whose sole purpose in life had been to make hers miserable, expected absolution?

"I have never given it a second thought," she said, as icily as she could muster.

"So, we're good, then?" asked Veronica.

Though Dodo was sorely tempted to lay out all her past grievances, she was loathed to admit how much Veronica had hurt her in the past, so instead she gathered the last vestiges of her patience and summoned a weak smile.

"Like I said. It's water under the bridge." Veronica was not worth wasting any more energy on…plus she was now pretty sure that her relationship with Rupert was quite recent and extremely tenuous.

Veronica shivered and pulled the cardigan tight around her narrow shoulders. "Are we done here?"

"One more thing. Did you happen to go down to the kitchen in the night and take some bread and milk?"

"Why ever would I do that? I need my beauty sleep."

A sharp retort sprang to Dodo's tongue but instead she asked another question. "Did you happen to borrow any wool from Bunty's stash?"

Veronica snorted. "Haha! That's even more strange. I thought you said you were good at this sleuthing stuff!"

Really, she is tap dancing on my last nerve.

Keeping her tone professional she snapped, "Some has gone missing. I thought I'd ask."

94

"Why would you think I'd taken it? Really Dodo, you disappoint me. Is that all?"

Veronica stood and made for the door but then returned and placed a condescending hand on Dodo's arm. "I really think you and I could be friends."

Dodo's jaw dropped at the nerve of the shallow, spiteful woman before her. She had not changed at all. She had probably come to Blackwood just to persecute her.

Dodo rustled up her patented smile, the one she reserved for manipulating men and said nothing.

Veronica squeezed her arm, then picked her way out of the room, humming. Her conceit knew no bounds.

Dodo suppressed a scream.

In your dreams!

§

Back in her room, Dodo felt an urgent need to bathe but there was no time for such luxuries. As a substitute, she let her irritations flush away by jotting all her thoughts down. There were several inconsistencies in Veronica's statement.

1. *If they are going to get engaged as she claims, why does Veronica not know Rupert's family?*
2. *If she has lied about her relationship with Rupert, perhaps she has lied about not knowing Walter. She certainly stopped herself from saying something.*

Dodo chewed the end of the chubby pencil she had found rolling around in the desk drawer.

3. *Isabella is right – two dead bodies is too much of a coincidence. Does this mean that Walter was pushed? If so, are the murders connected?*

Cut off from civilization and the help of the police, Dodo decided that she needed more clues if she was going to move further along in the investigation. She would need to search all the guests' rooms. Or rather, Lizzie would need to search them. Dodo would make sure that everyone was engaged after dinner giving Lizzie free rein upstairs.

§

"Poke around like a common thief?" said Lizzie, alarm radiating from her face. "What if someone catches me?"

"It's the only way," Dodo explained, as she put in her earrings. "I'll make sure to keep everyone in the drawing room after dinner. I would start with Veronica and Isabella's rooms."

"Even Mr. Bartie and Bunty?"

"Yes, even them." She touched a finger to her mouth, checking her lipstick. "We must be thorough. You can do Walter's room last since he certainly won't be coming back to his room."

Lizzie shuddered. "That's just spooky, that is. And a dead body lying in the room next door." Her lips had gone white.

"Oh, you'll need to do Granville's room too."

Lizzie gasped and clutched her chest.

"I know it's a ghastly task," said Dodo twisting on the dressing table stool to face her maid. "But without the ability to use police resources I can only solve this crime with more clues. I'll treat you to anything you want when we get home."

Lizzie's head lurched. "Anything?"

"You name it and it's yours."

"Silk stockings?"

"Done!"

The dinner gong rang out and Dodo checked her appearance in the mirror. Tonight, she had chosen to be warm in a clingy, fine knit, sapphire dress with a matching cardigan and floral silk scarf. Though the situation she found herself in was troubling, the elegant clothes helped her feel in control and professional.

"Give it ten minutes and then get started," Dodo said. "We will rendezvous back here at eleven."

§

Dinner was a subdued affair which was understandable given that there was a dead body upstairs and one out on the moors.

For a bit, Dodo was worried that Bunty would not come down, but she eventually appeared looking like she had put her finger in an electric socket. She was still wearing the same clothes from the morning.

Isabella was very quiet and had ditched the flamboyant dresses for a pair of flared wool trousers and a French sweater. Veronica on the other hand was woefully over-dressed again in a garish, fuchsia monstrosity with a huge lace collar.

All through dinner Dodo dropped hints about playing cards. No one protested, but no one agreed either. When dinner was over, she herded everyone into the drawing room like an efficient governess and pulled cards out of the drawer in the buffet before anyone could voice an opposition. She had taken the precaution of asking for card tables to be set up while they were at dinner.

"I just can't," moaned Bunty. "I'll sit here by the fire."

"Of course," said Dodo.

"And I just want to make a phone call for a taxi," blurted out Veronica. "As fun as this has been, I want to leave first thing in the morning." Her tone was cold enough to leave a thin frost on the furniture.

Dodo's blood ran as cold as Veronica's voice. She could not risk anyone leaving for fear that they would go to their room for some reason.

She was pretty certain that either the telephone would not work or that the taxi company would refuse to come out in the fog which still showed no signs of leaving but could she refuse to let Veronica try? Would it raise a red flag?

"Don't be too long," Dodo said. "Come straight back. We'll deal while we wait." She hoped the power of suggestion would encourage their hasty return with no detours and if not…well, that was not worth thinking about.

"Come on, Rupert." Veronica dragged him from the room in search of the telephone.

Dodo shuffled the cards, her mind on Lizzie creeping around upstairs. She dealt five hands as she waited, her foot jiggling with nerves, praying that Rupert and Veronica would not go to their rooms and interrupt Lizzie.

Bartie sat next to Isabella and jostled his chair close to hers.

97

"Without Granville's sponsorship I doubt that I will be able to make a name for myself here," Isabella said. "I'm thinking of sailing back to Spain."

"Oh, but that would be a terrible waste," said Dodo, tapping the tabletop with her nails. "Your voice is phenomenal. I have every reason to believe that I will see you at the Royal Opera House within a year."

Unless you are a murderer, of course.

Isabella raised hooded eyes. "Do you really think so?"

"I do. And besides, my father, Lord Alfred Dorchester, loves the opera and I imagine I can persuade him to sponsor you." Her nerves were so jumpy she was surprised she could continue to converse coherently. Every moment she expected to hear Veronica shriek like a fishwife.

Isabella's cheek hitched up in an attempt at a smile. "You would do that for me?"

"I would," assured Dodo, flicking her eyes to the ceiling.

"You *must* stay," pleaded Bartie.

The door burst wide open, and Veronica fell in. Dodo went limp with relief.

"The wire to the telephone has been cut," Veronica gasped.

Rupert was hard on her heels. "She's right! It's been cut!"

Chapter 15

A murmur of panic bumbled through the room as Dodo dashed out with Rupert and Veronica.

"Here!" said Rupert holding up a wire that had definitely seen the business end of a knife.

What does this mean?

Dodo stood thinking as her pulse pounded in her ears. "The intentional cutting of communication with the police does point to Granville's death being suspicious," she said carefully.

Veronica stared at her, crimson lips open. "Are you saying that there's a murderer in the house?" she cried, thrashing her arms around. "Then I refuse to stay a minute longer."

"And exactly how do you think you are going to get away?" asked Dodo, hands on hips, incredulous at the insanity of the comment.

Veronica bit her nail. "Oh." She looked sidelong at Rupert and took a step back. "It could be you," she accused him.

"For heaven's sake Vero, that is going too far!" Rupert complained. "I'm only here because of you. Why on earth would I murder a complete stranger?" He reached up to rub his neck in frustration. "I think it's time we told Dodo the truth."

The truth?

Veronica wrinkled her nose while shaking her head.

"Please no," she implored. Dodo had never heard her grovel and was bemused as to why.

"I think we must," Rupert continued. "I don't want anyone to suspect me as a murderer for one minute. That is not what I signed up for."

Dodo had stopped trying to understand.

Veronica's shoulders slumped. "Oh, alright!" She sucked in her cheeks and directed her gaze at Dodo.

"We are not a real couple." Her eyes dropped to the floor.

Ha! That would explain why I was getting mixed signals!

"I think you had better explain," said Dodo.

Rupert nodded at Veronica and leaned against the wall, hands in both pockets.

"Bunty mentioned that you were her cousin at the polo match—that part is true. And she may have mentioned that you were coming down because of a breakup. It seemed too good an opportunity to pass up. The idea of seeing you disappointed in love and arriving here with a thoroughly knock-out chap to make you green with envy. I couldn't resist and came up with a plan on the spot. I knew that Rupert might be"—she flashed her eyes at him— "convinced to play along and approached him about pretending to be my boyfriend. He owed me a favor as it happened." The scarlet rash creeping up her neck was evidence of the toll it had taken for Veronica to admit this.

Dodo clapped her hands together. "So, you and Rupert are not in a relationship which is why you know next to nothing about him or his family."

Veronica stared at her shoes. "Yes."

"That makes a lot more sense but why on earth go to all that trouble? What does it matter to you what *I* think?" asked Dodo flicking her gaze to Rupert who was struggling against a grin.

"Because fate handed me the opportunity to kick you while you were down, and I couldn't refuse."

Dodo was speechless at this blatant admission of utter malevolence.

"Rupert was reluctant at first," Veronica continued, oblivious of the storm she had created inside Dodo. "But his sister got into a bit of trouble with the law, and I asked Daddy to take care of it— he has friends in high places. I reminded Rupert that he owed me."

Dodo glanced at Rupert who nodded in confirmation.

"Perhaps it was beneath me," Veronica went on. "But I just couldn't resist. And there's no harm done, is there?" The smile on Veronica's face was so insincere that Dodo imagined her skin cracking.

Dodo blinked slowly while gripping her wrist to stop herself from slapping the infuriating woman.

"Since everything you both told me during the interviews is a lie, I need to start back at the beginning," she said.

"Not everything," contradicted Rupert. "We did wait out the ramble in the shed."

"Alright, but Veronica, you came here with the sole intent to humiliate me and Rupert, you came to settle a debt?"

"That about sums it up," he agreed.

Dodo pointed a finger at him. "What about the contretemps with Walter?"

"Just keeping up appearances." He ran a finger along his eyebrow. "It's how a chap would react to defend his girl."

Dodo's mind was reeling, and she began to pace.

"So, you two are outliers. Anomalies. That either complicates things or makes them easier. I haven't decided yet."

"Well, you better get that famous brain of yours in gear," spluttered Veronica. "I cannot abide staying here with a killer."

"The others will wonder what's up if we don't go back soon," pointed out Rupert, tapping his watch.

Lizzie!

She prayed that no one had left the drawing room. "Absolutely! Let's go!"

Veronica grabbed Dodo's arm. "Do you have to tell everyone else about our little sham? It's bad enough that we had to confess it to *you*. I can't bear everyone knowing."

"I won't mention it, but I imagine the truth will get around and it will serve you right," said Dodo, not trying too hard to push down the feelings of revenge and glee that slid into the hallway and danced a little jig on the back of Veronica's mortification.

They walked back to the drawing room and everyone stopped talking and looked up.

"The line has definitely been cut," Dodo confirmed. "Clean through."

"So, we are stuck here with two dead bodies and no way to contact the police," said Isabella, her voice hollow.

"I'm afraid so," Dodo affirmed. "And this complication confirms that at least one of the deaths is murder. Possibly both."

She watched as fear clouded every face in the room. "I didn't voice my suspicions before because I wanted to protect you all from alarm, but now that we know the phone line had been deliberately damaged, I can reveal that I believe Granville was smothered with a pillow."

Bunty let out a shriek. "But who would do such a thing and why?"

"That is the salient point," agreed Dodo.

"Why did you not tell us this earlier?" demanded Isabella.

"I apologize for the deception. I thought it was in your best interests to remain innocent of the fact until the police arrived. But now my hand has been forced."

And I didn't want to put pressure on the killer.

Bunty put the pieces together. "You mean that someone here is a murderer."

They were all sitting on the furniture around the fire, darting accusatory glances at each other.

"Mama mia!" said Isabella. "I am frightened."

Bartie took her hand. "I will protect you."

She slid her hand from his. "How do I know that *you* are not the murderer?"

Bartie's childlike eyes creased with pain.

"Everyone is overly emotional right now," said Dodo. "This is a shock, but let's not point fingers. It is late and I suggest we all go to our rooms and lock the doors for the night." Dodo wrapped her cardigan more tightly around her. "I need to consider the evidence without interruption. Tomorrow I will go over my conclusions with everyone at breakfast."

§

Lizzie had gone to fetch her things at Dodo's request that she spend the night with her. They were now locked in Dodo's room, bits and pieces that Lizzie had found in her search, laid out on the bed in the little brown bags, and a written list in her hand.

"Firstly," began Lizzie, "before I forget, Miss Isabella's passport has a great deal of recent German stamps in it."

"An opera singer might well perform in Germany," said Dodo with a mouth shrug. "So, on the surface it's not suspicious, but it might be worth looking into. Should be an easy enough topic to bring up in normal conversation."

"And, Mr. Danforth did not have any personal items, such as a picture of Miss Shufflebottom—" Lizzie raised her eyebrows.

"Ah, I can explain that," said Dodo and recounted Veronica's bluff and the reason Rupert had gone along with it. "But who knows what kind of trouble his sister got into and perhaps Walter or Granville found out about it and threatened him. It does not let him off the hook in my opinion."

Lizzie let out a mirthless laugh. "She came here just to rub your nose in your misfortune? What a horrible person!" She was brim full of loyal indignation. "But I can't see Mr. Danforth getting violent."

"That's because you have a crush on him and are letting that cloud your judgment," warned Dodo.

Lizzie clasped her hands to her lips. "I suppose you're right," she admitted. "You think I've let his looks get in the way."

"If he were a lazy-eyed, toothless sailor would you be giving him the same benefit of the doubt?" asked Dodo.

Lizzie pouted. "Point taken."

Dodo wrote down that she needed to ask Rupert about his sister.

"What about Veronica the Vengeful?" Dodo asked.

A deep giggle erupted from Lizzie. "That is quite an accurate title, m'lady."

"Oh, I have more," Dodo announced. "Veronica the Venomous. Veronica the Vindictive."

Lizzie wiped her cheek and clutched her stomach. "Oh stop! Stop!"

When she had regained her composure, Lizzie referred to her list. "Miss Veronica uses sleeping draughts and laudanum."

"Laudanum?" Dodo repeated. "I was wondering how someone could smother Granville without him lashing out and making a noise. It would be quite straightforward if he was sedated —even a woman could do it. But what connection does Veronica have to Granville? There again, I think I have to doubt everything she says. I couldn't trust her an inch at school, and I certainly shouldn't begin now."

She scratched a note about the laudanum. "What about Bunty?"

Lizzie screwed up her face. "You don't really suspect your cousin of killing the man she loved, do you?"

"No, but I've been wrong before. People change. He did seem rather keen on Isabella. Perhaps Bunty became violently jealous."

"It seems unlikely," said Lizzie. "And I didn't find anything incriminating in her room."

"Good! I should hate it to be her. And Bartie?"

"Speaking of Isabella, I found quite a few newspaper clippings about her in his room," she said with a wry grin, "and several dirty plates."

"The phantom food thief!" declared Dodo.

"It would seem so."

"Anything in Granville's room?"

"Other than him being stone cold dead in there, you mean?" Her brows were knit so tight Dodo had to fight back a grin. "I kept thinking he was going to sit up and ask me what on earth I was doing. I was so jumpy. Those silk stockings were the only thing that kept me going."

"You are an absolute angel!"

Lizzie clamped her lips into a pseudo-smile. "Yes, well, flattery will get you everywhere and no, I didn't find anything else in his room that could be considered a clue."

"Is that it?"

"No, m'lady. I've saved the best for last." Lizzie steepled her fingers and her eyes grew wide. "Mr. Montague's room." She picked up one of the brown bags.

Dodo jerked her eyes up. "Go on."

"I found a hint of red yarn on the floor, just wisps of it, but I'd swear it was the same color as the stuff you found in Granville's room. Why does it keep showing up everywhere, I'd like to know? And there were food crumbs in *his* room too. He must have got hungry that first night.

"There was an old bus ticket for somewhere in Cornwall dated a few weeks ago in one of the pockets of a jacket hanging up in his wardrobe and…" she paused, eyes dripping with satisfaction, "in the ashes of the fire I found some scraps of paper." She tipped one of the bags and out fell some charred flakes. "One looks like the corner of a photograph. It hasn't quite burned all the way. You can still see the corner of a man's pocket with a badge on it. I couldn't make it out though. And the other looks like a certificate or official document of some sort."

Dodo poked the flakes with her finger. "That is all very interesting Lizzie. Perhaps you have earned *two* pairs of stockings."

"I wouldn't say no. I shall call it hazard pay!" Lizzie said, casting a sidelong look at her mistress. "But that's not all. His room was a veritable treasure trove of clues. Remember how someone mentioned that he had a lot of luggage for a weekend? Well, I looked in both his suitcases. One was empty, the things hung in the wardrobe, but the other was half unpacked and contained another set of clothes *in a completely different size.*"

Dodo tipped her head. "Clothes in a different size? Why on earth—"

Lizzie rubbed her hands together. "I think I have the answer to that, m'lady. On his dressing table I found some Arabic gum, the kind my sister Annie uses when she performs in the theatricals in the village, and some light orange strands of hair." Lizzie stared at Dodo expectantly.

Dodo was completely flummoxed. "What do you think it means?"

"I think our Mr. Montague was wearing a disguise."

Chapter 16

"A disguise," said Dodo, drawing out the words and tapping her chin with the pencil. She thought back to her first impression of Walter; pot belly—that could easily be faked, bad teeth—could have been false, unkempt hair and beard—obviously a wig, and that thoroughly obnoxious, honking voice. All of it could be explained if he were acting a part.

"No one really knew Walter. He was a hanger-on," she continued. "He insinuated himself into the game in Cornwall. Then he showed up at the local pub and invited himself to Blackwood for the weekend. Who was he *really*? Why did he want to be here this weekend?"

"Whatever his motives, the poor man is dead, so does it really matter?" Lizzie pointed out.

Dodo scratched her head. "That's true, but his reason for wanting to be here is important. He must have had some ulterior motive or there would be no need for the disguise."

"Do you think his death was an accident, m'lady?"

"That's a good question and one I do not have an answer for. If it was a simple accident— and let's not forget that the moors claim lives every year—then it is unconnected to the murder of Granville. But what if the murderer saw through Walter's disguise and recognized him. The murderer might feel that he had to get rid of Walter to protect himself." She slapped her thigh. "What if Rupert saw through the disguise and the confrontation is what Isabella heard when he and Walter were arguing?"

"So, we are back to Mr. Danforth being the murderer," muttered Lizzie with little enthusiasm.

"Walter was using a disguise for some nefarious reason, perhaps Mr. Danforth uses his good looks for evil purposes. He certainly has a knack for disarming people. Different ends of the same stick."

"But why would Mr. Danforth want to kill Walter *or* Granville?"

"This is when a working telephone would be so helpful," Dodo declared, puffing air through her lips. "I really don't know. I need more evidence."

"Perhaps someone pushed Walter Montague and Granville saw them and started to blackmail the murderer?" suggested Lizzie.

"Too many theories!" cried Dodo, throwing her hands in the air. "I wish I could bounce my ideas off Chief Inspector Blood." She thought of the brooding, devastatingly handsome, single chief inspector and her heart caught in her chest.

Lizzie quirked a disapproving brow.

No! After their 'moment' Dodo must keep her distance from him.

"Well, with the phone down, you can't even bounce your ideas off Constable Plod," said Lizzie.

"You do have a knack for brevity, Lizzie."

"I try, m'lady," said Lizzie with a roguish grin.

Dodo picked up the burnt portion of photograph. "Let's get back to concrete evidence." She examined it. "The jacket looks like a blazer with a coat of arms. I think this might be the uniform for a gentlemen's club or a sport's team," she said bringing the picture closer.

"Great! That narrows it down to almost every gentleman in England," remarked Lizzie.

Dodo fingered the other piece of paper. It was charred brown from the flames. She held it up to the light and could just make out some print and a bit of handwriting next to part of a seal.

An idea popped into her head.

"Do we have any glycerin?" she asked Lizzie.

"I always have some in my first aid kit," Lizzie responded.

"Smashing! Then I believe I can make a solution that will bring out the print and handwriting from the charred paper."

Lizzie's curly head jerked back, and her brows shot up. "How on earth—"

"Chemistry class was where I first learned of it and then I perfected the method when Felicity Hardcastle burned a poison pen letter in the common room fireplace before I had a chance to look at it. I managed to rescue a singed piece and used the method

107

to find out who had written the letter." She laughed. "It's ironic that the writer was none other than Veronica the Vengeful. Felicity had told on her to Miss Clemence, the mathematics teacher, and Veronica was exacting her revenge."

"She sounds like a thoroughly rotten sort!" exclaimed Lizzie.

"She is. Look at why she is here this weekend. What kind of person does that?"

"An unhappy one," said Lizzie. "Mark my words. Miserable people seek to make others feel as bad as they do. That's where the proverb about misery loves company comes from."

"Perhaps."

"Doesn't all that we've discovered mean that Mr. Danforth is available?" asked Lizzie with a glint in her eye. "What better revenge than to pinch Veronica's pretend beau!"

"How delightfully wicked!" said Dodo. "But I must remind you that we were considering him a candidate for the murderer not five minutes ago." Dodo squeezed her eyes shut. "And I came here to get away from men. Let's agree that he's off limits, shall we? I have work to do."

Lizzie smoothed the eiderdown. "If you say so."

Dodo slid off the bed with the delicate charred paper in her hand and placed it on the desk. "I trust you also have rubbing alcohol in that first-aid kit. If not, we'll have to use gin."

Lizzie dug around in her bag and held up a small bottle of alcohol in triumph.

"Excellent. Now we need two parts water, five parts alcohol and three parts glycerin. I'll use the glass for water by my bed as a crude measuring cup."

"You have quite the memory," stated Lizzie.

"I may have used the method more than once," said Dodo with a wink.

She poured the different liquids into the bowl on the occasional table, mixed it around with a finger and then laid the paper on the top.

"Can you grab one of the bedside lamps and bring it over here, please."

Positioning the light, Dodo and Lizzie bent over the bowl and watched as the print started to become visible.

"'Cor!" exclaimed Lizzie. "It's like magic!"

"Drat! I need some paper. Keep watch Lizzie!" Dodo grabbed the notebook from the bed and rushed back to the bowl.

"-icate number 437654," read Lizzie.

"Certificate! Death, marriage or birth? We may never know. But the number might help. When the fog lifts, the police could look into it with Somerset House, the national record office."

Dodo kept watching to see if the solution could bring out the handwriting. "It's a number," she gasped. "1895. What's that, twenty-eight years ago?"

"Why would Mr. Montague burn a certificate?" asked Lizzie.

"Perhaps it contained his real identity. Since he was in disguise, everything we know about him is phony. He would need to burn it so that he remained undiscovered."

"Then why bring it at all?" said Lizzie.

"The more we learn, the less things become clear. The only things we know for sure are; one, that Walter was a male in his late twenties—"

"Ooooh, that certificate is from twenty-eight years ago," pointed out Lizzie. "Perhaps it *is* his birth certificate."

"Could be." Dodo held up two fingers. "Secondly, we know that Walter invited himself to this weekend and disguised his appearance. The why is still a mystery." She added a finger. "And third, we know that he has disappeared, presumed drowned."

"It's been three days. I think we can safely say he is departed," said Lizzie with a frown. "We also know that he burned these things in the fire. That makes four solid facts."

"Quite right, Lizzie."

Dodo pulled the piece of paper from the solution to dry on the table.

"Ok, let's move on to what we know of the others." She looked at her notebook. "Why does Isabella go to Germany so often? There could be a quite straightforward explanation, but she could also be a spy."

"A spy!" cried Lizzie. "A little, pretty thing like that! No!"

"What do you imagine spies to look like? Old men with hooked noses and dirty raincoats? No, she would be the perfect candidate for a spy. Her career makes frequent travel unsuspicious, and her appearance is disarming. As you say, she does not look threatening in the least. And what do we know of her family and their politics? Nothing. There is currently a military dictatorship in Spain and there are factions who are opposed to this. What if there are Spaniards who are seeking German sympathy? It's not impossible. We live here in our little bubbles and forget that there is political unrest elsewhere."

"Blimey! I never think like that," gulped Lizzie.

"But how can I find out about any of it?" Dodo gestured with her hand. "Say, Isabella, what's with all those trips to Germany? Furthermore, that would reveal that we had snooped in her room. But it's information I can keep in my hip pocket. Suppose Granville and Walter were politically active and she was tasked with eliminating them?"

"Oh, now that is too much! Sounds rather far-fetched if you don't mind my saying so," pronounced Lizzie.

Dodo hitched up one side of her mouth. "It does, but one never knows." She tapped the notebook with the pencil. "Who's next. Miss Shufflebottom and her drugs. She could have drugged Granville and then smothered him."

"She certainly could but why? What motive does she have?" asked Lizzie.

"Motive. Always a tricky thing," replied Dodo. "Perhaps she and Granville had a torrid affair and he threatened to tell Rupert."

They both giggled at the absurdity.

"But remember, Veronica claims she did not know Granville was coming. She only knew that *you* were coming," said Lizzie. "And her relationship isn't real so she wouldn't care about blackmail."

"Drat! That's right!"

"But perhaps you can ask her if any of her sleeping powders are missing," said Lizzie as she fluffed the pillows on the bed.

"Oh, now that *would* be useful. Five points to Lizzie."

Dodo grabbed the notebook again.

"Right then. Questions that need answering. One, is Veronica missing any laudanum or sleeping draught? Two, what political persuasion is Isabella and why does she go to Germany so often? Three, who *is* Walter Montague? What was his real name? Four, does anyone recognize the crest on the blazer in the picture?" She underlined the word 'blazer' and scribbled 'Bunty' beside it. "Five, why are bits of Bunty's missing wool showing up all over the place? And six, who cut the blasted telephone wire?"

Dodo chewed the pencil. "Money is often the motive, so I think there is one more question. Now that Granville is dead and his father is close to dying, who stands to inherit all that money and the title?"

Chapter 17

As the grandfather clock struck midnight, Dodo rapped on Bunty's door with Lizzie at her heels. Lizzie had not wanted to venture out and her anxious eyes were snapping left and right in case the murderer struck.

"Who is it?" said Bunty, her tone strained. In the space of forty-eight hours, her voice had lost its innocence.

"It's me. Dodo."

A key turned in the lock and Bunty, looking like a kitten that had been rescued from a drowning, let them in, locking the door tight behind them. "Can't be too careful."

"Quite!" agreed Dodo. "Now, Lizzie did some poking around while we were all downstairs and found some interesting clues."

Bunty's brow tried to rise with indignation, but sorrow was the victor and she just appeared confused. "Should you do that? It seems rather underhanded."

"Of course we should. How else will we discover who…well, you know?"

Dodo sat in one of the scruffy chairs. "Now, we have been using our noggins and we have some questions for you. Are you up to it?"

"Fire away." The monotone reply was not encouraging, but Dodo sympathized. Grief was a prickly companion.

She decided to start with a startling piece of information to awaken Bunty's faculties. "Walter was not really Walter."

"What?" Bunty's drooping face revived a touch.

Dodo let the next arrow fly. "He was in disguise."

For the first time, Bunty's facial muscles really got into the game. "Disguise? How do you know?"

"Lizzie found some Arabic gum and strands of orange hair in his room."

Bunty's lips formed an 'o'.

Dodo took this as a positive sign of mental engagement. "I actually feel better that his voice was not really that affected. He was so boorish. I suppose that was an act too. I had to stop myself from slapping him," said Dodo with a small grin.

Bunty's large hands pushed back her bushy hair. "Why on earth would he do that? What can it mean?"

"That part is still a mystery," admitted Dodo. "And now he is dead, so we cannot ask him."

A shift in Bunty's eyes indicated that the wheels of her reasoning were beginning to grind. "Do you think meeting him at the card game was not by chance? Did he stalk Bartie like a deer?"

"It would appear so. The question is, why did he need to be present this particular weekend and why did he have to practice subterfuge to do it? Any ideas?"

Bunty scrunched her lips. "Money? Bartie did inherit the estate. It's quite large but Walter would have no way to get his hands on it, surely?"

Dodo spread out her palms. "What if Walter married you?"

Bunty's eyes slid to the side. "Well, then if Bartie died, I would get all the money since he is not married and has no children. But I was to marry"—her voice cracked—"Granville."

A motive tickled at the edges of Dodo's brain.

She pulled the burnt fragment of photograph from her pocket and laid it in front of Bunty. "Does this mean anything to you?"

Bunty picked it up and brought it close to her eyes. "Can you bring me that lamp," she asked. Her vision narrowed then she slapped the picture down. "It is the crest of Granville's cricket club."

Dodo moved to the edge of her seat. "So, this could be a picture of Granville?"

Bunty wiggled her nose. "Well, I can only say that it's someone wearing a blazer *from* the cricket club. There are hundreds of members. Where did you find it?"

"In the fireplace in Walter's room."

Bunty's eyes bulged reminding Dodo of a frog.

"For arguments sake, let's say it *was* a picture of Granville," continued Dodo. "Why would Walter need it? Did he know that Granville was going to propose perhaps? Was his plan to get Granville out of the way so he could propose to you for your money?"

Bunty's lips began to tremble. "I didn't even know that Granville was going to propose so how would Walter know?" Her eyes filled with tears as she studied her ring. "Walter would have to kill Bartie as well."

"And there's a big hole in that theory, m'lady," said Lizzie. "Mr. Montague drowned *before* Granville was… murdered." Lizzie said the last word in a stage whisper, tipping her head toward Bunty who was staring at her hands.

"Oh! You're right! This is making my head hurt," said Dodo, resting her forehead against her palms. "Perhaps I need to sleep on it all, let everything stew overnight and hope it all looks clearer tomorrow."

"And what about the laudanum, m'lady?"

Lizzie was in top form tonight, firing on all cylinders.

"Oh, yes. Veronica brought both laudanum and sleeping powders with her. They could have been used to sedate poor Granville."

Bunty choked. "So, you are saying Veronica killed Granville?" Her face was misery personified.

"No, no," assured Dodo. "At least I don't think so. But the mention of the drugs made me realize that if someone used such a thing on Granville it would have…made their task easier. A post-mortem would tell us."

Bunty wiped her nose with an oversized man's handkerchief. Dodo noticed it was embossed with a letter 'P'.

"Do you happen to know anything about Isabella's politics?" asked Dodo.

"Goodness, Dodo! I can hardly keep up with you." She gave her nose a good blow. "I don't think Isabella has any." She pushed the tangled mass of hair behind her ears. "What has that got to do with anything?"

Dodo took a deep breath. "Lizzie found her passport. There are lots of visits to Germany, that's all."

"Oh Dodo, really! Looking through my guests' personal things?" The soiled hankie was now in a pile on her lap.

"This is an investigation! It is absolutely necessary if we are to find out who killed poor Granville."

Bunty slumped and placed her chin on her fist. "I suppose you're right, but it seems so dishonest."

Dodo tipped her head gently to the side to indicate to Lizzie that it was time to leave. "Crime solving is a dirty business, darling. Sometimes one has to get one's hands dirty." She jumped up. "Well, we'll be off then."

Bunty's chin began to tremble again. "I wish I could wake up to find it has all been some ghastly nightmare. It's at times like this that I really miss Mummy."

Dodo kissed her forehead and gave her hand a squeeze. "Of course. Now, try to sleep, darling."

§

The atmosphere at breakfast was tense. Everyone throwing sharp, suspicious glances like magician's knives, at each other. They were still cut off by the sabotaged phone, but the fog was giving signs of lifting. Dodo felt hopeful.

Now that the truth about Rupert and Veronica was out, they were not even sitting next to one another and Dodo was almost sure that she had caught Rupert studying her before he snapped his eyes back to his fried eggs. Knowing the whole tale allowed Dodo to put her prejudices aside and look at him through different lenses. That he had agreed to come with Veronica out of brotherly concern for his sister was a point in his favor. And she had to admit that the curve of his jaw was quite alluring. But such pontifications were ill-timed, she reminded herself.

"Did everyone sleep well?" she asked to kick the quiet group into talking. "I have to admit I had to take a sleeping draught."

"I always take them," murmured Veronica, looking much worse for wear. "I can't sleep at all otherwise."

"Oh really," encouraged Dodo, being careful to keep her tone conversational. "What brand do you use?"

"*Dr. Mac's* usually but I must not have packed enough and had to use an old chloral hydrate I found at the bottom of my suitcase. Though I could have sworn I packed plenty."

Missing some perhaps? Now that the ball was rolling in the right direction, it was time to dig some more. She buttered some toast.

"Someone introduced me to *Mrs. Packer's Sleeping Draught* last year in Germany," she lied, poking the bear again. "I find Germany takes such a toll on me. Don't you agree, Isabella?"

Isabella frowned. "I'm sure I would not know," she said with a clipped voice.

"Oh, pardon me!" said Dodo. "I thought someone said you traveled to Germany recently. My mistake."

Isabella nodded vaguely and became very interested in her food.

"When do you think we will be allowed to leave?" asked Rupert. His voice reminded her of hot chocolate on a cold night.

"Well, the police will want to question everyone as soon as the roads clear. It looks more promising today. And they only know about Walter missing, since the phone has been dead since the second death."

Veronica grumbled.

After breakfast most of the group tried reading. Dodo decided to go to the kitchen to talk with the cook about the missing food. Although it seemed evident that the culprit was Bartie, she felt that it was a lead worth checking out.

The row of heavy copper pots hanging on the wall and the smell of baking brought a rush of happy childhood memories. The room was bustling with oodles of energy, and the warmth of the ovens threw out a wave of welcome heat. Mrs. Brown, her craggy, kind face rigid with concentration, was busy making scones for tea. One could almost forget the terrible things that had happened. Almost.

"Hello, Mrs. Brown."

"Hello, Miss Dodo." She brought her flour-dusted hand to her cheek. "I hope you don't mind me still calling you that? That's who you are to me. Always will be."

116

"Of course not!" Dodo had enjoyed many a treat in Mrs. Brown's comforting kitchen.

"Can I get you something, m'lady?" Her iron gray hair was neatly rolled at the base of her neck, but small ringlets had escaped around her ears in the moist air.

"No, thank you. I had an enormous helping of your delicious kippers for breakfast. I'm very comfortable."

Dodo pulled out a chair.

"What about all this nasty business?" said the cook. "I hardly slept a wink last night and I locked my door."

"Yes, it is rather awful. I'm hoping to make some headway in the case while we wait for the police to arrive."

"Bunty told me about your sleuthing." The cook pulled some more dough from a cracked bowl that was covered with a striped dishtowel. "Says you've been in the papers. Well, I never!"

"I've been involved in a few cases. Mother hates me doing it, but I must confess I love it. Not the danger, of course, but putting the clues together. However, I usually work with the police."

"Too dangerous for driving right now," Mrs. Brown said as she rolled out the dough for a pie. "We get a blanket fog that refuses to budge like this, every few years. What we need is a good storm to blow it all away."

"And soon!" Dodo watched as the cook expertly wielded the heavy, marble rolling pin over the dough. "Would you mind if I asked you a few questions?"

"Of course not," she said, placing a dish over the pastry crust and cutting around the edge with a knife.

"Bunty mentioned that some food has gone missing."

"Yes, some farmhouse cheddar, bread, and a few other bits."

"I think I may have discovered who it was," said Dodo. "Bartie admitted to some late-night snacking."

The knife stopped. "Oh no. Couldn't be. Master Bartie doesn't like farmhouse cheddar, it's much too strong for him. He prefers those mild French cheeses, like brie."

Not Bartie?

117

"Was it just the first night then?" Dodo asked, remembering that Lizzie had mentioned crumbs on the floor of Walter's room.

"No. Seems like each morning more is missing and with this fog and the blasted phone down I can't re-order." She tutted.

"Oh, then I shall continue my quest to find the culprit."

Dodo rubbed her hand along the polished oak table while Mrs. Brown pinched the edges of an apple pie, and they talked of the old days for a while.

"I remember that time Miss Bunty got into the molasses in her white Sunday dress," said Mrs. Brown, wiping her hands on an ancient apron. "There was no getting that stain out. I still think she did it on purpose. Poor Lady Gillingsworth. She was such a dainty, feminine lady. I think she had trouble understanding her daughter."

Dodo recalled the day well as she and her sister had been visiting. "Yes, Aunt Olivia used to lament that Bunty should be more like Didi and I. But one can't change one's nature, can one?"

Mrs. Brown walked over to the oven and popped in the pie. Dodo's mouth began to water. "I can smell ham for lunch but what deliciousness have you planned for dinner?"

The back door blew open suddenly, revealing a windblown, vigorous Rupert Danforth. The damp fog had turned his fair waves into tiny curls that clung to his forehead.

"I say, Lady Dorothea, I think I've found something you might want to see."

§

Dodo rushed to the mud room, grabbed a mackintosh that was hanging by the door, and followed Rupert out into the fog. The confounded stuff had thickened again, and she despaired of it ever lifting.

Rupert explained as they walked. "I came out to retrieve the glasses that we left here the other day—don't want to be an ugly guest—and they were gone, but I found something that wasn't here before."

He opened the door to the garden shed and kept his hand there while ushering Dodo in. Her hair brushed his chin and sent a pleasant ripple down her spine.

She saw nothing in the shed and looked at Rupert in confusion.

"Over there." Rupert pointed under the window. "A glass. It's not one of ours and it was not here before."

Dodo picked up the glass using the bottom of the mackintosh. Despite the fact that the police were unable to be here to take prints, it was vital to preserve evidence that could be used later. She held the dingy object up to the dim light and caught a whiff of spoiled milk. There were actually a lot of print smudges on the glass.

Perhaps I should ask Father Christmas for a fingerprint kit this year.

Dropping to her knees she examined the ground. "Did you and Veronica eat bread out here?" she asked.

"No," he responded. "Just the brandy."

Dodo was acutely aware of his presence above her but commanded herself to attend to the matter at hand. She pushed her finger into one of the crumbs and lifted it up. Cheese!

"Any cheese?"

"No food at all."

"And you are sure this glass was not here when you and Veronica were hiding out?"

He pointed to the spot where the glass had been. "I'm sure. We huddled on the floor by the window for a while. If that glass had been there, I would have had to move it to make room to sit."

And it couldn't have been here when Lizzie came to retrieve the glasses, otherwise she would have seen it.

Dodo fanned out her fingers and studied the rest of the area. A flash of red caught her eye, and she pulled a shovel away from the wall. Hidden under a rake and some gardening shears was a badly wound skein of scarlet wool. Her pulse kicked up a notch.

"And I don't suppose you brought this out either."

Rupert regarded the wool with surprise. "Absolutely not!"

He ran a hand through his damp hair which caused Dodo a moment of distraction. "What do you think it means?" he asked.

119

Concentrate, Dodo.

"I think it means that someone had the same idea as you. They used this shed as a hiding place. But why? And who?" Cogs were churning in Dodo's brain like a combine harvester, and she bit her lip in concentration.

She struck the wall of the shed.

"What?" cried Rupert. "Have you had a breakthrough?"

Dodo narrowed her eyes. Rupert may not be the scoundrel she had first thought him to be, but she did not really *know* him.

"How do I know I can trust you?"

He ran his tongue over his lips as she dragged her eyes up to his astonishingly blue eyes.

"Look, I know a little of the history between you and Veronica," he began, stuffing his hands in his pockets and looking down at his shoes.

Alarm bells sounded. "If your only source is Veronica, I doubt that you know much truth about it at all," she said. "Let's just say she put me through the wringer at school and leave it at that."

Rupert kicked the floor. "Actually, she was pretty honest because she desperately needed me to come along with her for this little ruse." He looked up. "She's terribly jealous of you, you know."

Dodo snorted and examined his exquisite face for signs of insincerity. She found none.

"It's true," he continued. "She told me that no one liked her at school, not really, and that you were always incredibly popular. She said it was utterly infuriating. It didn't seem to matter what she did, she could not inspire true friendship in people like you did.

Then to have to watch your star rise in the world of fashion was the absolute last straw."

Dodo could hardly believe her ears. *Veronica, jealous of her?*

"I had no idea," she said.

Rupert shrugged his shoulders. "Bumping into your cousin was just too much of a temptation for her. When Bunty mentioned that you were coming down to Blackwood to get away because you were upset, Veronica seized the chance to assert her dominance. To gloat at your expense."

"The shrew!" declared Dodo, her mind spinning.

After cracking his knuckles, he declared, "Couldn't agree more."

Dodo snapped her eyes up to his.

"Now I see what a petty harpy she is. If I had known…" He left the sentence unfinished.

"I am in complete and total shock," Dodo said, brushing her hair back from her face. "All I know is that Veronica made my life miserable at school and now you tell me she was jealous the whole time? I'm just trying to wrap my head around it."

Rupert took a small step forward and she felt her heart catch.

"She also told me you made her feel like a failure and this was a chance to get her own back. She painted such an awful picture of you that I agreed to her terms. But now that I know you…"

Rupert's kindness and proximity in the small hut were definitely stirring up something inside her. Should she let her guard down while she was so vulnerable? She had been disappointed in love so many times recently. Could her heart stand another blow? Did she even want to take the risk?

"Veronica bullied me constantly."

Rupert took another step forward and her resolve lost its teeth.

"It's because you make her feel insecure. She's always wondering what you will wear and what you will say."

Dodo could smell his fruity cologne and inconvenient bolts of attraction were crackling in the air between them. She took a breath. "Really? I find that hard to believe. She put me in my place more times than I can count at school."

He advanced so that she had to tip her head back to see his playful eyes that were a thousand different hues, and for an instant she forgot completely where they were.

"Well, these days her confidence is at rock-bottom," he said, his voice soft and ragged. "I probably shouldn't tell you this, but that's why she uses the old laudanum—it gives her Dutch courage." The vibrant blue of his eyes was burning hers, like staring into the sun for too long. "It's not just for sleeping," he continued.

She tried not to be affected by the mellow cadence of his words as they flowed over her like warm honey.

"She's a bundle of nerves most of the time." She watched as his eyes traced the edges of her face. "That's why she's so anxious to leave—she's running out and getting desperate."

Dodo shook her head in disbelief keeping her eyes fixed on his. This was a side of Veronica she had not expected.

"It's true," Rupert asserted, placing an arm on the wall behind her head and sending her reluctant heart skidding. "Her father told her that she needs to get help, or he will send her off to one of those sanitoriums in Switzerland."

He was talking about Veronica, but it was a cover. The tone of the words was as if they had been out to dinner and they were saying goodbye on her doorstep. Dodo felt herself succumbing to his magnetism.

What harm would it do?

"Is that the sort of trouble your sister got into?" Dodo asked, wondering where all this was going to lead.

The mention of his sister burst the mood as surely as if she had stuck a pin in him. His face sagged and he withdrew his arm. "Yes. Some bally bloke introduced it to her at a party. It's the very devil. She soon became addicted to the stuff and stole something while under the influence. She was arrested." He pivoted away from her. "It would have devastated my parents, so she came to me for help. I happened to be at a party with Veronica at the time and she told me her father could make it all go away..." He turned his head to look at Dodo. The eyes that were heavy with proposition just moments before were now clouded with pain. "If I agreed to come with her to Blackwood as her beau. It seemed a small price to pay and she made good on her word."

Dodo knew she would do the same and more if it were Didi who was in trouble.

The heavy dose of coquetry that had filled the hut had fled like a cockroach in the light. She ran her hands down her coat, unsure whether to be relieved or disappointed.

"And what do you think of Miss Shufflebottom now that you have spent several days in her company?"

Before he could control his reaction, a look of horror flashed across his cheeks, his eyes overflowing with undisclosed opinions. "Let's just say…only blackmail would induce me to spend another weekend with her."

Rupert was definitely growing on her.

His smile melted like wax on a candle. "She has made *one* more demand of me."

"Oh?" Dodo had the impression that the other shoe was going to drop.

His reply was a whisper that tickled her ear sending a riot of pleasure to her brain. "She has made me swear that I will not make a play for you."

Whatever Dodo imagined he was going to disclose, this was not it. She flicked her eyes up to meet his and found there a mixture of mischief and longing. The flirtation was back.

She pursed her lips. "And what did you say to that?"

The expression on his face transformed to assurance. "I told her that the terms of the deal had been met and that she had no further claim on me."

Was he saying he did *want to make a play for her?* The idea that had unsettled her not five minutes ago, now caused a bubble of excitement.

She looked askance, a wicked smile playing around her lips. "How did Veronica take that news?"

"She crashed about like cymbals at the end of a symphony, but I stood my ground."

His eyes blazed with triumph.

Her foot knocked the dirty glass bringing her back to earth with a bump.

"I –" he began.

She held her hand up to stop him. Enthralling as a confession of affection would be, the glass reminded her that a murderer was at large. Though such romantic advances were usually more than welcome, in the middle of a murder investigation it was a distraction that took one's eye off the ball. Besides, though she was decidedly attracted to the *real* Rupert, she couldn't be one hundred per cent sure he was not the murderer, at this point.

Looking at the glass she said, "I have a murder to solve. And so, we have circled back to the question of trust."

Rupert took a step back, hands raised in surrender, but he did not look hurt. "Fair enough. You mean, how can you know I didn't kill Granville?"

"Exactly."

"I can't prove I didn't do it," he said, leaning against the wall of the shed looking good enough to eat. "Just like anyone else in the house, I could have sneaked into his room and smothered him."

His candor was refreshing. She had expected him to make all sorts of protests about his innocence as people in the hot seat usually did.

He tipped his head so that a stray curl kissed his forehead. "What does your gut say?"

She blew a breath out through her mouth and considered him, hands on hips.

"To tell the truth, you do come across as a little shifty…" She couldn't control her lips as they curved into a seductive smile. "But I'm willing to give you the benefit of the doubt, for the present."

The best grin tickled his features and she had to swallow.

He stepped forward again. "I deem it an honor to have won a smidgen of your trust, m'lady." He brushed the wandering curl back and stepped closer again, causing her breath to catch. "You didn't like me at first, did you?"

Standing so close she could feel his breath. He was disheveled by the weather, his chipped tooth on full display and she remembered how she had felt when he first burst through the door with Veronica. She had merely judged him on the evidence she had been presented at the time.

Dodo lifted a carefully plucked brow. "You were with Veronica. Case closed."

The provocative smile faded, and he unexpectedly reached out to tuck her hair behind her ear. She flinched with pleasure as his fingers grazed her skin.

124

"Veronica was that bad to you?"

"Worse!"

He drew his thumb across her chin, and she struggled to keep her breathing even. "And you thought, of all the girls in the world I had picked *her* as a girlfriend. Now it all makes sense. Do you think any better of me now?"

She lifted her finger and thumb with barely an inch between them. "A little."

He dropped the hand from her face and raising himself to his full height, placed the palm to his expansive chest. "On my honor, I declare that Veronica is the exact opposite of the type of girl I would choose, and that I did not kill Granville Post. I had never met the man before."

She bit back a grin. "Oh, all right. I believe you."

Rupert bowed deep like a cavalier. "Hallelujah!"

He leaned, and she held her breath thinking he was going to kiss her on the mouth. When he planted a chaste kiss on her cheek, she felt like a runner who experiences the thrill of winning the race only to learn they have been disqualified.

Pull yourself together, Dodo.

"Now, I'd like to help if I can," he said.

Dodo did not need time to consider his proposition.

"Alright. Here are some of the mysteries I am working to solve. Some food has gone missing from the kitchen, enough for Mrs. Brown to mention it to Bunty. A red ball of wool has disappeared from Bunty's stash, which we have now found out here along with some crumbs and a cup, and"—she lowered her voice—"I have discovered that Walter was not Walter."

Rupert frowned. "Okay, I was following until the last bit."

"Walter was wearing a disguise. Fake beard, wig, false teeth. I think he padded his middle too."

"Golly! Why on earth would a chap do that? But it does explain his inappropriate comment about Veronica. At the time I didn't think he really meant it. I just felt I had to react the way I did as part of the hoax. And that awful voice! It sounded like bagpipes with a sore throat!"

"What a brilliant description!" agreed Dodo.

125

"But what does his disguise have to do with this glass and the red wool?"

"It's not totally clear to me yet, but it is beginning to make sense. Walter disappeared after the ramble. The next morning Bunty and I went in search of him and found his hat at the top of a cliff and his scarf floating at the bottom, but *we did not see a body.*"

Rupert rolled his hands. "And you think he may have faked his death in the same way he faked his life, used the yarn to find his way back, and been hiding out here stealing food from the kitchen to survive."

Spreading her arms as wide as the crowded little shed would allow, she exclaimed, "Very good, Mr. Danforth. That is exactly what I'm thinking."

"It is an ingenious theory, Lady Dorothea," he said, and Dodo felt warm at his praise. "But why?"

Again, his quick mind had got to the heart of the matter.

"I haven't put all the dots together yet, but I think it has to do with Granville and Bunty getting married. And Bartie's money. It almost always has to do with money."

"Always?" He quirked a brow. "Do you do this sort of thing a lot?"

She tucked the other side of her hair behind her ear and saw his eyes follow her hand. "More than you might imagine. It has become quite a hobby of mine."

She put the wool in one hand and looked at the glass she had placed on the floor.

"Use my handkerchief," said Rupert, offering her a clean, folded piece of linen. She wrapped the glass and put it in the other hand and moved to the door, but as they both stepped over the threshold, Dodo caught her shoe and tripped into Rupert's side bringing his face dangerously close to hers and setting every nerve tingling.

His strong arms gently pushed her upright.

"Sorry."

"Not at all." His voice was low, and smooth. "It was a pleasure."

She paused, trying to pack all the emotions he had unleashed back into their box so that her brain could process the facts of the case.

As they walked back to the house, Dodo felt the need to discuss all the thoughts that were whirling through her mind. Vocalizing her ideas often helped things fall into place and now that she trusted Rupert, she decided that two minds were better than one.

"My maid found a piece of a burned photograph in Walter's grate that may have been of Granville, and a charred piece of a certificate from 1895. If I can figure out why he had those things with him, I think I can solve the case."

"Is Bartie worth *so* much money?" His stride was long and sure, and she had to trot to keep up with him.

"Not as much as Granville, but very wealthy."

Rupert chuckled. "You'd never guess."

"I know. It's one of the things I love about them. Bartie and Bunty are that rare breed who do not need fancy trappings to be happy."

"So, let me see if I have this straight. You now believe that Walter murdered Granville. How does that get him Bartie's money?"

As she had hoped, in laying things out for Rupert, the wheels of her understanding were turning as smoothly as those on a steam train. The hazy picture was coming into focus.

"Walter must have heard or suspected that Granville was going to propose, but he had set a plan in motion to marry Bunty himself…" Her mouth dropped open in horror. "Then he would arrange a little accident for Bartie and Bunty would inherit. Perhaps he would murder her too."

She picked up her pace. "Quick. Let's hurry."

"Why?" said Rupert, jogging to keep up.

"Because now that I believe Walter is alive, the only thing standing between him and the money is Bartie!"

Chapter 18

While Rupert digested that fact, Dodo heard a noise. Her whole body tensed with concentration.

"Did you hear that?" she asked him.

"No. What?"

"I thought I heard someone close by," she whispered. She could only see about five feet in any direction.

They both stood still, straining to hear.

"I must have imagined it," Dodo said. "I've spooked myself." She started to head toward the house when she thought she heard another noise. A hiccup? "Was that you?"

"Was what me?"

"I heard a hiccup." She scanned the area around her as her skin prickled. Was she being paranoid or was someone really watching them? Walter?

"Could it have been an animal?" asked Rupert.

Dodo replayed the sound in her mind as she stared into the curtain of fog. "I suppose so," she admitted. "Goodness. I must be jumpy if I'm hearing things."

Relieved to be in the relative safety of the house, Dodo relaxed.

"Well, I should rush these up to my room," said Dodo, indicating the glass and wool. "Can you watch Bartie for me? I'm nervous about his safety."

"Of course," said Rupert, ducking into the drawing room.

Dodo ran up the stairs two at a time with a light heart and found her maid making the bed.

Lizzie slammed her hand to her chest.

"Oh m'lady!" she gasped. "You could give me a bit of a warning before you plunge in like that. With this murder unresolved I'm skittish as a cat."

"Sorry," said Dodo holding up the items from the shed. "Look! We found some more clues."

"We?"

Dodo ignored the question. "Where is my magnifying glass?"

"In the desk drawer," said Lizzie pointing.

Having reclaimed it, Dodo held the glass to the light and looked through the magnifier. Something was stuck to the bottom and she turned it upside down.

A single, red hair.

Fear gripped her by the throat. "Walter is definitely not dead," she whispered.

Lizzie paused as she smoothed the bedding. "Of course he is. You and Bunty saw his scarf in the bog and the skid mark at the top of the cliff. And he's been missing."

But the seed of doubt that had been planted in the shed, and by the sounds she heard as they walked back, was growing like a tropical plant in the hot houses of Kew Gardens. Images of red wool, cut wire, white feathers, burned papers, and now a red hair on the bottom of the glass, played on a loop in her head.

Dodo fell down onto the newly made bed, convinced that her theory was headed in the right direction but with the clear feeling that she was still missing something.

"This glass was found in the garden shed *after* Walter's disappearance," she began, the spoken words helping her reformulate her theory. "After," she emphasized.

Lizzie stopped hanging Dodo's clothes. "And you are sure?"

"Absolutely!"

Dodo explained how Rupert had found the glass and swore it was not there when he and Veronica had taken refuge in the shed.

"And you did not see it when you retrieved their glasses, did you?" she asked Lizzie.

The dress she was hanging slipped to the floor. "No."

"It wasn't in plain view, but you would definitely have noticed it." Dodo sat up on the bed staring at the ghost-white Lizzie.

"Oh," Lizzie said, looking around with wide eyes as though Walter were hiding somewhere in the room ready to attack.

"If, as I now believe, Walter is alive," said Dodo, slipping off the bed and pacing as she talked, "he would easily be able to move about at night because everyone believes he is dead. He could have cut the telephone wire and killed Granville."

Dodo lifted up the red yarn. "Here is what I think happened. Let's see if you can find holes in it."

"Alright." Lizzie sat in the chair, gripping the arms, as Dodo paced.

"Walter Montague, or whatever his real name is, was desperate for money. He learned that Lord Gillingsworth was a wealthy, single man with an unmarried sister. He formulated a plan to marry Bunty but somehow heard that she had met someone who might propose. He had to act to prevent that marriage. He created a disguise to meet Bartie and went to Cornwall with the design of introducing himself to my cousin, as Walter.

"Weeks later, he somehow discovers that Granville is coming to Blackwood for the weekend, shows up in Devon, 'bumps' into Bartie and Bunty and inveigles an invitation. His aim from the beginning was to kill Granville, reappear in Bunty's life in his true identity, marry her, and then kill Bartie so that Bunty would inherit."

"Kill Mr. Bartie?" cried Lizzie in horror.

Dodo raised the yarn again. "Walter was the one who suggested the ramble, but he doubled back in the fog and hid, waiting for everyone to return. I suggest that he then re-entered the moors with the yarn so that he would not get lost returning and staged his fall into the bog by throwing his scarf down and hiding his hat in the long grass. Then he followed the yarn back, rolling it into a ball as he went, and hid in the shed."

All the pieces of the puzzle were falling into place as she marched around the room.

"After everyone went to bed, a very hungry Walter entered the house to get some food and milk. He went up to his room to remove his disguise and burn any incriminating documents. I don't think he had ever met Granville in person and needed the photograph to identify him. Then, he went back to hide out in the shed, intending to kill Granville the next evening."

The more she talked the more she liked the theory.

"Walter probably witnessed Bunty and I going to search for him and relay the news that he was missing, possibly drowned. Just as he planned. It was all part of his plot to kill Granville."

"That's how he cut the telephone wire too!" gasped Lizzie.

"Yes! He didn't want the police to arrive before he could make his escape. The fog was a complication he could not have foreseen, and it meant he would probably not be able to leave the estate after committing the murder."

Lizzie shuddered. "He could have found me snooping in his room!"

"But he didn't. Let's not scare ourselves with 'what ifs'."

She stopped her pacing and sat on the chair facing Lizzie. "Before we all came to bed the following evening, he either used a sleeping draft or laudanum that he brought or stole from Veronica and put it in the glass of water on Granville's nightstand. Then he waited for it to take effect, smothered the poor chap while he slept, and then slipped back to the shed."

Lizzie stared, mouth open. "It does explain everything— almost."

"You mean the certificate?"

Lizzie nodded.

"Perhaps it was not a vital record certificate. Perhaps it was another way to verify Granville's identity."

Dodo clasped her hands under her chin. "We are *so* close. I can feel it," she cried. "But since Walter is still alive and dangerous, we need to set a trap. He remains a threat to Bartie."

"You and your traps," Lizzie moaned. "They terrify me."

"Would you feel better if we involved Mr. Danforth?"

Lizzie's eyes widened and the concern melted from her features. "Oooh, I'd feel much better," she agreed. "Do I take it he is out of the doghouse?"

Dodo recounted all that Rupert had told her.

"I *told* you he was a nice person," Lizzie declared. "You can't look like an angel and be a devil."

"Lizzie, you do worry me," said Dodo, laughing. "I think you had better have me vet all your beaus. You are so easily led by a handsome face—it could get you into trouble."

Dodo took a deep breath. "Getting back to the matter at hand…the trap. Walter still needs food and water. I say we wait for him in the kitchen tonight. He has no idea that we believe him to be alive so his guard will be down."

"I think I'm going to regret this," Lizzie wailed, biting her lip.

§

The grandfather clock in the upper hall struck twelve and Dodo shifted to prevent her foot from going to sleep. Rupert, Lizzie, and she were hiding behind the pie cupboard in the kitchen. They had already been there for thirty minutes and Dodo was beginning to get pins and needles.

As she was rubbing her leg to get the circulation flowing, quiet footsteps approaching put them all on alert. Dodo peeked around the cupboard ready to fight, but sank back down, finger to her lips in warning when she discovered that it was just Bartie and Isabella.

Lizzie clamped her hand to her mouth to stop from giggling and Rupert bit his knuckles.

"What do you fancy?" said Bartie, clicking on a light.

The three of them shrank back as far as they could, which meant that Dodo's side was now smashed up against Rupert. Not a completely unpleasant situation. In fact, a familiar sensation of attraction began to unfurl.

"What do you have?" Isabella's silky voice sounded…sultry.

The unmistakable sound of Bartie gulping filled the silence and Dodo broke into a smile.

"Uh…we…that is to say…uh, gosh! I can't think straight." Bartie laughed as a slight shuffling could be heard. "I say," he said, "steady on."

"But I like you, Bartie."

Lizzie slid her eyes over to Dodo with a confused grin.

"You do? I thought, well it doesn't matter what I—" Bartie was silenced by what could only have been a kiss.

"You have been so brave in the face of all this unpleasantness," Isabella continued at last, her accent thick and heavy. "I feel unafraid when I am with you."

The screech of a chair sliding on the tile, shattered the quiet, and Lizzie and Dodo jumped. Rupert put a comforting hand on Dodo's shoulder, and she realized she had not thought of Chief Inspector Blood in quite some time.

"I say," Bartie crooned. "I would do anything to protect you Isabella."

The kitchen fell quiet again.

Rupert shifted slightly. His nose inadvertently touched Dodo's hair sending a hot spark through her.

"I would like to see you again, Bartie," said Isabella. "Perhaps we can arrange to meet at your friend Arthur's?"

"Arthur?" From the tone it was clear Bartie was baffled.

"Arthur Milton. I think you said he works in government or something. You mentioned him yesterday."

"Oh, you mean Arthur Mulberry."

"Yes, Mulberry. That's right. I think you said he has a large lake on his property, no? I am eager to go boating with you. It would be fun. Romantic." She rolled the 'r' as only a Spaniard can.

"Of course," breathed Bartie, his voice ragged. "Anytime."

"Then that is settled," she purred. "Now, is there any of that delicious cake left from tea?"

"It will be in the pantry," said Bartie, his voice fading as he moved.

A clatter as the plate hit the table and the clink of cutlery, told the three hidden spies that the pair were gathering items.

"Let's go and sit by the fire embers in the drawing room," suggested Isabella. "It will be more…comfortable."

The light switched off and the door closed amidst a bout of juvenile giggling from Dodo and Lizzie. Rupert shook his head with a smile.

"I didn't see that coming," he chuckled.

"He has been like a love-sick puppy since she arrived," said Dodo.

"Well yes, but she didn't seem at all interested."

133

"That much is true," Dodo agreed. "Something must have changed." She was thinking of her advice to Bartie to be more subtle.

Finally, the threesome could spread out a little, but Dodo immediately missed Rupert's warmth.

Lizzie was still shaking with mirth. "What an unlikely pair, if it is not out of place for me to say so."

Rupert chuckled. "I agree wholeheartedly," he whispered.

"Poor Bartie," began Dodo. "I think she is—"

The hinges of the kitchen door squeaked, and they all shrank back into the shadows. Almost silent footsteps slowly padded across the flagstone in the dark. Dodo risked another peek. This time she saw the indistinct shape of a man and withdrew, eyes wide in warning.

They all waited, adrenaline flowing, as the person poured some milk and foraged for food.

Dodo was bracing herself to jump out when another set of footsteps approached from the hallway. The shadowy figure ducked under the old kitchen table with the milk and food as the person opened the door again. He retrieved a bottle of wine and some glasses, humming happily.

Bartie.

The light from the hall reflected the panic in Lizzie's eyes.

No one moved for a full three minutes after Bartie's departure, including the dark figure under the table. Dodo's pulse pounded in her ears as her heart hammered in her chest.

Then the intruder crawled out from under the table and tiptoed to close the door, but not before the light bathed his features. It was a very different face to the Walter she knew; dark, close cropped hair, even teeth and no pot belly.

He crept back to the table and picked up the bread.

Now was the time.

"Stop!" cried Dodo as she bolted upward in the darkness like an uncoiled spring. Rupert ran to guard the door and Lizzie stood, face taut, gripping her scarf.

Walter looked left to right, clearly considering an escape route as Dodo yelled, "Lights!" and Rupert flipped the switch.

Any color that Walter's skin may have possessed drained, and he grabbed a bread knife from the table, brandishing it like a sword.

In a brilliant move, Lizzie threw an apple at Walter's head that clipped his temple, causing him to lose focus for a second and giving Rupert the opportunity to fling himself onto Walter. This knocked the knife to the floor. Dodo ran to retrieve it, then moved to guard the door.

After a brief tussle that had Dodo's heart in her throat, Rupert managed to roll Walter onto his front, pinning his hands behind him. Expletives flooded from the man's mouth as he struggled.

"Quick! Throw me the rope!" shouted Rupert, panting from exertion.

Lizzie had hidden the rope in a corner of the kitchen under a basket and threw it to Rupert who strung Walter up like a Christmas turkey.

The kitchen door suddenly hit Dodo in the back, pushing her forward as Bartie and Isabella crowded into the room.

"What the—"

Chapter 19

When Bartie and Isabella first clapped eyes on the scene in the kitchen, they were speechless.

Walter continued to swear until Lizzie threw Rupert her scarf to use as a gag and then he frog-marched the unmasked Walter into the drawing room.

Dodo offered a quick explanation of the situation to the bemused couple and suggested that Bartie run and rouse the others for the full dénouement.

Veronica stumbled into the drawing room clearly under the influence of a sleeping aid. She squinted against the harsh overhead lights, her unnaturally blond hair in a state of deshabille.

Registering Walter, she slurred, "Who is this strange man and why is he tied up?"

"Sit here, Veronica, and all will be revealed," suggested Rupert in a soothing voice. Complying, she shuffled over to the sofa and collapsed against the arm.

Bunty arrived next, red-eyed and more wild-haired than usual, sporting a large, flannel nightdress that resembled a Ringling Brothers circus tent. Her eyes darted around the room finally resting on the captive.

"What's going on? Who is this?" she demanded.

"Look harder, darling," said Dodo. "Look at his eyes."

Bunty peered at the gagged and bound stranger, whose eyes were flashing with anger and humiliation. "I'm stumped," she finally said.

"This is the man we all know as Walter," said Dodo, to gasps all around.

"But Walter is dead," said Isabella.

"That is what he wanted us to believe," explained Dodo. "That way he could prowl around unfettered and execute his dastardly plan."

"Which was?" asked Bartie.

"Do *you* want to tell your story?" Dodo asked Walter, whose eyes were now narrowed to slits. A purple bruise was blossoming nicely on his forehead from his short trip to the kitchen floor.

Walter shook his head, struggling against the rope.

"Alright then, I shall tell it," declared Dodo. "Walter Montague is a fake name. Actually, everything about the Walter we met was fake." She glanced around the room. She had everyone in the palm of her hand—everyone except Walter, that is.

"Interested in Bartie's inheritance, this man put into action a diabolical, premeditated plan to come to Blackwood this weekend with the sole purpose of murdering Granville."

Hushed murmurs invaded the room.

"But why?" wailed Bunty.

"Because Granville stood in the way of his fortune."

Walter stopped struggling.

Dodo laid out the rest of her theory.

"Hence the elaborate ruse with the false teeth, hair, beard, and padding. The final touch was the odious personality. How am I doing?" She flicked her gaze to Walter, who merely grunted and hunched his shoulders.

"Yes, he's the one who suggested the walk on the moors," cried Bunty, pointing a finger. "I would have waited for the weather to be better. I remember now that I suggested playing dominos instead, but Walter insisted."

Walter was studying everyone.

"He did not anticipate the fog of course, which unfortunately for him, did not lift. If it had, he would be long gone," said Dodo.

Isabella spat something in Spanish, causing Veronica to stir.

"Whaaat is…" Before finishing the sentence, her head sagged in slumber again.

"How did you catch him tonight?" asked Bunty.

"We hid in the kitchen," Dodo replied. "We knew he had to get food at some point."

"But why did you have to kill Granville?" asked Bunty through round tears that splashed down her cheeks. "Bartie's money would never come to you."

137

"His plan was long term," explained Dodo. "He couldn't have Granville propose and mess things up, so he had to go.

"Later, Walter would reappear in your life as his true self, court, and marry you. After a suitable time had passed, he would execute the second murder. Bartie would have an *accident* and then the money would come to you."

"Murder my beloved brother?" cried Bunty in horror.

Walter shifted his shoulders indicating that he wanted to speak. Dodo nodded and Rupert removed the scarf from his mouth. A sound like the Devil himself laughing, erupted from Walter.

"You think you're so clever," he spat, squeezing his left eye shut, stirring a memory in Dodo. "But you've got it all wrong." Gone was the honking, nasal voice replaced with an ordinary baritone filled with venom.

Dodo snapped her fingers.

"He's right!" she agreed, as the final piece slipped into place. "It was not Bartie's money he was after. It was Granville's."

Walter froze.

"The certificate was not Granville's. It was yours. It is the vital piece of evidence. And I am sure you have another copy somewhere safe."

"I don't understand," said Rupert.

Dodo pointed at Walter. "You are Granville's close relative. Probably an illegitimate half-brother. Am I right?"

Walter locked eyes with Dodo and then stared at the ground.

"On the first night, I noticed Granville had the odd habit of squeezing one eye shut when he found something funny or strange. Walter has just made that same expression." She looked at Lizzie with triumph. "It *was* a birth certificate you found. It was *Walter's!*"

Walter sighed which was as good as an admission.

"I see it clearly now," Dodo continued. "Similar height, similar build— which you went to great lengths to disguise."

"Can you explain it for those of us who are less brilliant," said Rupert with a wink.

"I am now proposing that Granville's father had an affair at some point and his mistress had a baby boy, a boy that would have a legal claim on the Post estate if Granville died.

"Walter's mother was probably paid a handsome amount to keep quiet and go away or risk retribution. But at some point, she must have mentioned it to her son. I suspect Walter was very curious about his father and researched him only to find that the man was ailing and very, very wealthy.

"Riches beyond Walter's imagination were within reach. He deserved that money for having been rejected. Only Granville stood in the way."

"That's right!" howled Walter, finally breaking his silence. "I was made to feel ashamed, prevented from meeting my father. And there was Granville living in the lap of luxury while Mother and I lived in a hole of a place in Watford. We deserved some compensation."

Rupert crushed the raging man in a bear hug and Bartie replaced the gag as Walter wiggled and thrashed.

"Walter found his birth certificate which listed Granville's father," resumed Dodo. "Not using his title, but instead his Christian name I would guess, and he formulated his scheme.

"If he could get rid of Granville, when his ailing, natural father passed away, Walter would present himself, with his birth certificate, as the legal heir and inherit the lot. Walter probably studied the society pages and magazines to learn all about his half-brother and his habits, which was how he knew who *I* was. Then somewhere along the way Walter heard that Granville wanted to marry. He had to speed up his plan and stop the marriage before a son and heir was born."

"You stole my only chance at happiness," sniffed Bunty. "My only chance."

"With the fingerprints from the glass I found and the rest of the evidence we have gathered, there should be enough to convict him," said Dodo.

Walter hung his head.

"If you promise to behave, I am prepared to let you have the last word," said Dodo.

Walter nodded and Rupert removed the scarf.

139

"My father gave my mother a large settlement when I was born which she burned through in no time. As a boy, we barely had enough to live on. I was teased relentlessly at school for my frayed blazers and old shoes. Mother kept her promise not to reveal who my father was, but I badgered it out of her when she was drunk one day, about a year ago. When I learned the truth, I was furious. I felt no loyalty to the man who had abandoned us and refused to recognize my existence, hiding me away like refuse." His voice had risen in pitch and volume.

Veronica roused again and murmured, "Why am I...," before slumping against the arm of the couch once more.

"What is your real name?" asked Isabella.

"Clarence Williams. It's my mother's maiden name. I wouldn't use that—"

Rupert replaced the gag.

"I say we lock him in the wine cellar until the police get here," said Rupert.

"I second that!" declared Bartie.

Both men stood and wrestled Walter—Clarence—away.

Bunty watched, rocking back and forth, her hands clasped to her chest.

"Your reputation as a detective is well earned," said Isabella, when the men had gone.

"Thank you," said Dodo, "but I have to tell you that I have learned more things in the course of my investigation, things that might not please you so much."

Isabella quirked a brow, lips puckered in suspense.

Dodo lowered her voice to a whisper. "I found something that has led me to the crazy conclusion that you might be a German spy."

Isabella's olive skin paled.

"You are half right," she said, lowering her voice and drawing Dodo to the back of the room. "I am a British spy. I bring back information to your government from Germany and Spain. I am on *your* side."

Dodo chuckled. "So, the date with Bartie to the lake...?"

"...was to pass information to a government official, Arthur Mulberry, outside of Whitehall. Making that date was the very purpose of my visit to Blackwood but everything else that happened complicated things. My contacts knew that Bartie was friends with this official and encouraged me to develop a relationship with your cousin. I was not enthusiastic about the mission, but I must confess that I have grown very fond of Lord Gillingsworth." Her smile was soft and genuine. "He is so authentic and kind. There are not many men like that in the world."

"I couldn't agree more," said Dodo.

Rupert and Bartie trooped back in.

"He won't escape from there any time soon," said Rupert, coming to stand by Dodo.

Veronica lifted her head, eyelids heavy with sleep.

"I'd better get her back to her room," Rupert said.

Dodo watched as he lifted Veronica's arm around his shoulder. She felt a twinge of something that was suspiciously like jealousy.

She went to sit by Bunty as a distraction and held her hand as the first shards of dawn sunlight began to pierce the darkness. She snapped up her head and was relieved to see that the fog had finally lifted.

"At last!" she exclaimed.

When Rupert returned, she watched as he scanned the room. When their eyes met his face lit up and her heart squeezed in her chest.

"I say," he said, sitting so close to her that she could feel his thigh through her skirt. "Perhaps after all this we can catch a play or something."

After the excessive tension of the last few hours and the lack of sleep, Dodo laughed uncontrollably at the normality of the question.

I must be punch drunk.

"I thought that would break the terms of your contract," said Dodo with a wicked smile when she had calmed down.

"Ah, but you forget, I told Veronica that I have satisfied the conditions of our contract and she is in no position to oppose me in her current state. I think I might just drop her off at a rehabilitation clinic on the way home. She is wasted."

141

He leaned toward Dodo and her blood quickened, but a thundering knock at the door made them start.

Chapter 20

Lizzie, who had been sitting quietly watching all the actors in the drama, now rushed to answer the door.

The deep rumble of an insistent male voice, and the murmur of Lizzie's short replies, indicated to Dodo that the police had arrived. A short man with a mustache and a copious amount of pomade in his gray hair, filled the doorway to the drawing room.

"This is—" began Lizzie.

"I am Inspector Turner," he interrupted. "The report of the missing man reached me several days ago and this is the first time the fog has lifted sufficiently to allow me access to the estate." The inspector laid heavy emphasis on every third, or fourth, word causing Dodo to choke back a smile. He was certainly no Chief Inspector Blood.

"As you see," the country inspector continued. "I have come at the first opportunity." He doffed his hat. "Who made the call?"

Dodo stepped forward, hand extended. "It was I, Inspector. Lady Dorothea Dorchester."

The inspector glanced at her hand as if it were a snake, then remembering his manners, shook it. "What is the status of the missing man?"

"He is no longer missing, Inspector."

The policeman's jaws flapped, and undecipherable mutterings crossed his lips. He eventually composed himself enough to say, "So this was all a waste of time?"

"On the contrary, Inspector. We do have a dead body upstairs and the culprit is locked in the wine cellar."

The squinty, dark eyes widened. "Indeed?"

"Have a seat, Inspector. We will tell you the whole story while my maid fetches some tea."

§

The wreckage of the tea and toast lay on the occasional table and the inspector was wiping his brow after listening to the incredible tale.

"By gum!" he declared. "You did a fine job, m'lady."

Dodo had the good graces to appear flattered. "I do have some experience in these matters." She resisted mentioning her association with Scotland Yard.

"This evidence, the charred documents, and the tumbler...I suppose you still have them."

"Of course. I understand about the chain of evidence, Inspector Turner." She tipped her head to Lizzie. "Would you mind terribly?"

Lizzie disappeared.

"Now, I suppose I should retrieve the murderer," said the inspector.

"I can take you," said Rupert, who had sat by Dodo's side the entire time.

The inspector followed him out of the door to the cellar.

Isabella approached Dodo. "Thank you for withholding my secret," she said.

"It has no bearing on the crime in question," Dodo assured her. "So, I did not think it relevant."

"All the same," began Isabella. "I am in your debt."

"Nonsense! I will just expect VIP seating at your next performance." Dodo touched Isabella's arm.

"Of course!"

"And a promise that you won't break Bartie's heart."

Isabella's features fell. "You're right. Though I am really quite fond of him, there can be no future for us, and Bartie is such an innocent. I shall break things off before they get too far."

Too late.

Lizzie entered holding the evidence in a bag.

"Thank you, Lizzie," said Dodo.

"Thank you for all the credit you gave me," she replied.

"Your work was critical to solving the crime, my dear," Dodo retorted. "Without your snooping we would still be at square one."

144

Lizzie's cheeks matched the color of the roses on the bone china teacups.

A shuffle by the door caught Dodo's attention. Walter, or rather Clarence, was resisting the inspector.

"Easy now!" barked the no-nonsense inspector. "You can make this difficult for yourself or not. Up to you. And watch your tongue—there are ladies present!"

The strength of the scowl on Clarence's face could have peeled the paint from the walls. He had clearly not appreciated his time in the dark wine cellar.

Someone touched Dodo's shoulder and she turned.

Rupert.

"Clarence is not amused that we left him down there," chuckled Rupert. "His language made even the inspector blush."

"Captured murderers are seldom happy," remarked Dodo, still conscious of the spot Rupert had touched.

Two constables took Clarence away and the inspector approached her.

"Here is all the evidence, we gathered, Inspector," Dodo said. "I should point out that my fingerprints might be on the milk glass, though I tried not to handle it."

"That is quite alright, m'lady. I'll tell the technical boys about it." He touched his hat. "That trick with the glycerine—I'm still tickled by that bit of genius." He took her hand and kissed it. "It has been a real pleasure meeting you, Lady Dorothea."

"Likewise," she replied.

"If I have any further questions…"

Dodo gave him her home phone number.

"I will see you in court," he said, turning to leave.

"Absolutely."

For a heavy-set man, the inspector was surprisingly light on his feet and almost skipped out of the house.

"I have met girls with unusual hobbies before, but yours takes the biscuit!" said Rupert, grinning like a schoolboy.

Their gazes collided. He was looking at her as if she were the only girl in the world and it felt good.

He took a step closer, setting her senses alight.

"Do you make this sleuthing a regular habit?" he asked, taking her hand.

"I do love a good mystery." He was now so close she could see wisps of white floating in his perfectly blue irises. "And murder just seems to happen when I'm around."

He moved even closer, and her heart clamored in her throat.

"So being a friend of yours can be dangerous," he said, staring straight at her lips.

"A f-f-friend?" she stuttered, feeling his warm breath fan her skin.

Rupert's lips puckered as he considered, filling her with longing.

"Well, I don't want to make assumptions that I have no authority to make," he said slowly, tracing her jaw with his finger so that she tingled from head to toe.

"You will have to explain yourself, Mr. Danforth," she whispered.

"This weekend has been complicated..." he began.

Dodo chuckled. "It's been more than that!"

"Quite." He placed her hand against his chest. "Look, I need to get Veronica home, she's in no condition to travel alone."

Dodo raised her brows.

"She *did* help my sister," he said by way of explanation. "I owe her that much."

Dodo brushed the tip of his nose with her finger. "You are just a very thoughtful man, Mr. Danforth."

Rupert's face creased with pleasure. "If you say so."

Dodo laced her fingers through his.

"As soon as I get Veronica sorted out, I'll call you," he said.

She tipped her face up. "I shall look forward to it." He dipped his head but before he could kiss her, a familiar, irritatingly shrill voice came from near the door.

"I have had the oddest dream," Veronica said, looking as though she had been to the same hairdresser as Bunty. Lipstick was smudged all across her chin and every inch of her was wrinkled.

Glancing in their direction, Veronica jolted awake.

"What is going on here? Rupert!"

146

The End

I hope you enjoyed this cozy mystery, *Murder on the Moors*, and love Dodo as much as I do.

Interested in a free prequel to this series? Go to https://dl.bookfunnel.com/997vvive24 to download *Mystery at the Derby*.

Book one in the series, *Murder at Farrington Hall* is available for $.99 on Amazon. https://amzn.to/31WujyS

"Dodo is invited to a weekend party at Farrington Hall. She and her sister are plunged into sleuthing when a murder occurs. Can she solve the crime before Scotland Yard's finest?"

Book two of the series, *Murder is Fashionable* is available for $1.99 on Amazon. https://amzn.to/2HBshwT

"Stylish Dodo Dorchester is a well-known patron of fashion. Hired by the famous Renee Dubois to support her line of French designs, she travels between Paris and London frequently. Arriving for the showing of the Spring 1923 collection, Dodo is thrust into her role as an amateur detective when one of the fashion models is murdered. Working under the radar of the French DCJP Inspector Roget, she follows clues to solve the crime. Will the murderer prove to be the man she has fallen for?"

Book three of the series, *Murder at the Races* is available for $2.99 on Amazon. https://amzn.to/2QIdYKM

"It is royal race day at Ascot, 1923. Lady Dorothea Dorchester, Dodo, has been invited by her childhood friend, Charlie, to an exclusive party in a private box with the added incentive of meeting the King and Queen.

Charlie appears to be interested in something more than friendship when a murder interferes with his plans. The victim is one of the guests from the box and Dodo cannot resist poking around. When Chief Inspector Blood of Scotland Yard is assigned to the case, sparks fly between them again. The chief inspector and Dodo have worked together on a case before and he welcomes her assistance with the prickly upper-class suspects. But where does this leave poor Charlie?

Dodo eagerly works on solving the murder which may have its roots in the distant past. Can she find the killer before they strike again?"

For more information about the series go to my website at www.annsuttonauthor.com and subscribe to my newsletter. You can also follow me on Facebook at:
https://www.facebook.com/annsuttonauthor

Agatha Christie plunged me into the fabulous world of reading when I was 10. I was never the same. I read every one of her books I could lay my hands on. Mysteries remain my favorite genre to this day - so it was only natural that I would eventually write my own.

Born and raised in England, writing fiction about my homeland keeps me connected.

After finishing my degree in French and Education and raising my family, writing has become a favorite hobby.

I hope that Dame Agatha would enjoy Dodo Dorchester at much as I do.

Acknowledgements

My proof-reader – Tami Stewart
The mother of a large and growing family who reads like the wind
with an eagle eye. Thank you for finding little errors that have
been missed.
My editor – Jolene Perry of Waypoint Author Academy
Sending my work to editors is the most terrifying part of the
process for me but Jolene offers correction and constructive
criticism without crushing my fragile ego.
My cheerleader, marketer and IT guy – Todd Matern
A lot of the time during the marketing side of being an author I am
running around with my hair on fire. Todd is the yin to my yang.
He calms me down and takes over when I am yelling at the
computer.
My beta readers – Francesca Matern, Stina Van Cott,
Your reactions to my characters and plot are invaluable.
The Writing Gals for their FB author community and their
YouTube tutorials
These ladies give so much of their time to teaching their Indie
author followers how to succeed in this brave new publishing
world. Thank you.

Printed in Great Britain
by Amazon